The Close-Up

Also From Kennedy Ryan

Reel: A Hollywood Renaissance Standalone Novel
A Hollywood tale of wild ambition, artistic obsession, and unrelenting love.
Directors. Actors. Producers. Costume Designers. Musicians. Writers.
A world where creatives make art and make love!

* * *

HOOPS Series
Available in ebook, Audio & Paperback
(Interconnected Standalone Stories)

Long Shot (A Hoops Novel)
Iris + August's Story

Block Shot (A Hoops Novel)
Banner + Jared' Story

Hook Shot (A Hoops Novel)
Lotus + Kenan's Story

Hoops Shorts (A Hoops Novella Collection)
Avery + Decker's Story
Quinn + Ean's Story

* * *

ALL THE KING'S MEN
Available in ebook, Audio & Paperback

The Kingmaker
Duet Book 1 - Lennix & Maxim
Kindle Unlimited

The Rebel King
Duet Book 2 - Lennix & Maxim
Kindle Unlimited

Queen Move
Kimba & Ezra

The Killer & The Queen - Coming Soon!
(Novella co-written with Sierra Simone)
www.subscribepage.com/TKandTQ

* * *

THE SOUL TRILOGY in Kindle Unlimited
My Soul to Keep (Soul 1)
Down to My Soul (Soul 2)
Refrain (Soul 3)

* * *

THE GRIP TRILOGY in Kindle Unlimited
Grip Box Set
All 3 Books in 1
In Kindle Unlimited
(includes exclusive BONUS material)

Or

Individual Grip Trilogy Titles
In Kindle Unlimited
FLOW (The GRIP Prequel)
GRIP (Grip #1)
STILL (Grip #2)

* * *

Before I Let Go
Skyland Book 1
Coming November 15, 2022

* * *

THE BENNETT SERIES
When You Are Mine (Bennett 1)

Loving You Always (Bennett 2)
Be Mine Forever (Bennett 3)
Until I'm Yours (Bennett 4)

The Close-Up

A Hollywood Renaissance/HOOPS Novella

By Kennedy Ryan

1001 DARK NIGHTS

PRESS

The Close-Up: A Hollywood Renaissance Novella
By Kennedy Ryan

Copyright 2022 Kennedy Ryan
ISBN: 978-1-951812-74-4

Foreword: Copyright 2014 M. J. Rose

Published by 1001 Dark Nights Press, an imprint of Evil Eye Concepts, Incorporated

Sign up for the 1001 Dark Nights Newsletter
and be entered to win a Tiffany Key necklace.

There's a contest every month!

Go to www.1001DarkNights.com to subscribe.

As a bonus, all subscribers can download
FIVE FREE exclusive books!

One Thousand and One Dark Nights

Once upon a time, in the future…

*I was a student fascinated with stories and learning.
I studied philosophy, poetry, history, the occult, and
the art and science of love and magic. I had a vast
library at my father's home and collected thousands
of volumes of fantastic tales.*

*I learned all about ancient races and bygone
times. About myths and legends and dreams of all
people through the millennium. And the more I read
the stronger my imagination grew until I discovered
that I was able to travel into the stories… to actually
become part of them.*

*I wish I could say that I listened to my teacher
and respected my gift, as I ought to have. If I had, I
would not be telling you this tale now.
But I was foolhardy and confused, showing off
with bravery.*

*One afternoon, curious about the myth of the
Arabian Nights, I traveled back to ancient Persia to
see for myself if it was true that every day Shahryar
(Persian: شهریار, "king") married a new virgin, and then
sent yesterday's wife to be beheaded. It was written
and I had read that by the time he met Scheherazade,
the vizier's daughter, he'd killed one thousand
women.*

Something went wrong with my efforts. I arrived in the midst of the story and somehow exchanged places with Scheherazade — a phenomena that had never occurred before and that still to this day, I cannot explain.

Now I am trapped in that ancient past. I have taken on Scheherazade's life and the only way I can protect myself and stay alive is to do what she did to protect herself and stay alive.

Every night the King calls for me and listens as I spin tales. And when the evening ends and dawn breaks, I stop at a point that leaves him breathless and yearning for more. And so the King spares my life for one more day, so that he might hear the rest of my dark tale.

As soon as I finish a story... I begin a new one... like the one that you, dear reader, have before you now.

Then

Takira

"How's the soup coming, Kira?" my mother shouts from the dining room. "It's done?"

I roll my eyes and sigh, but not too loudly because I don't want licks from Mama tonight, and she *will* pop me if provoked. Or toss the nearest shoe at me.

"Yes, ma'am." I lift the lid from the fish soup, drawing in a deep breath of the flavor-rich aroma and letting the steam mist my face.

"Good," she yells. "I hope we have enough of everything. All them boys'll be hungry."

The last thing I want to do in the middle of the week is help my mother prepare a full Trinidadian spread for twelve immature jocks. Bad enough I *live* with one. Now I'm cooking dinner for Cliff's basketball team instead of watching *Vampire Diaries*.

I survey the dishes, pots, and pans of food splayed across every surface in our kitchen. In addition to the soup, we have curry crab and dumpling, pelau, salt fish, coconut bread, aloo choka, rice, and every other Trini dish Mama had time to make.

"Go upstairs and check on your brother," Mama says, the faintest lilt of the islands languishing in her words even though she's lived in America nearly twenty years. "He lolling off. His friends be here any minute, and he not even down here."

I grumble under my breath but turn the soup off and cut through the living room to climb the stairs. My hand is on the handle to open the door, but I catch myself just in time. Growing up, Cliff and I were closer to each other than to my sister Janice, who is four years older than him and five years older than I am. Cliff and I are what some call Irish twins, born only 13 months apart.

Ain't no child of mine Irish nothing, Mama always says. Instead we're her "Trini twins."

Still, the days when I could barge into Cliff's room unannounced are long gone. You interrupt a boy's quiet time with his bottle of lotion in one hand and his dick in the other, you learn to knock *quick.*

"What you want?" his newly deeper voice demands from the other side of the door.

"Um, I *want* to be watching *Vampire Diaries,* but I'm cooking dinner for your friends. Mama says come down. The team'll be here soon."

The door opens, and my own dark brown eyes stare back at me from more than half a foot above. Not only are we "Trini twins," but we could be fraternal as much as we look alike, despite the dramatic height difference. We have the same high cheekbones, though mine are set in the rounded curves of my face and his are more pronounced. Identical clefts in our chins passed on from Daddy. Heavily lashed eyes under a thick, dark slash of brows. Well, mine *were* thick before I experimented with wax and tweezers last week. Right now they're what's left.

"Help me with this tie," Cliff says, turning back into his room, leaving me to follow inside. He holds out a tie with the word "fabulous" stitched into the burgundy and gold pattern of his private school's shield of arms.

"Isn't this from your school uniform?" I frown at the altered tie.

"Yeah, but we had Kenneth's mom sew the 'fabulous' on for the starters, kinda like Michigan's Fab 5."

"Won't you get in trouble for changing it like this?"

"We're about to give St. Catherine's its first state championship," he says, his smirk cocky, his tone assured. "We could stitch *suck my dick* on that tie, and the headmaster wouldn't care. Long as we bring home them Ws and sponsor dollars."

"I still don't get how a high school has corporate sponsors."

"It's a private school cranking out top athletes. You wouldn't understand with that basic public school education you getting," he teases.

"You cried like a little bitch when St. Catherine's recruited you and Mama said you had to leave all your friends and accept that scholarship. So watch who you call basic, bruh."

"I did not—"

I cut him off with a *who you trying to fool* look, and he grins, showing off the straight, white smile my parents are still paying for.

"Okay, maybe I cried a little at first," he concedes. "But that was sophomore year. It was worth it. Look at us now. 'Bout to be champs."

I snatch the tie from him and motion for him to bend. We were the same height—five nine—until his freshman year in high school. Over that summer, he shot up in a growth spurt of more than five inches. He grew a few more to reach his current height of six feet, six inches.

"Why you wearing a tie anyway?" I ask, looping it deftly. How I know how to do this and he still doesn't is beyond me. "For dinner at the house?"

"We're taking some pictures. Capturing the road to our championship." He frowns down at me, his smile flattening into a line. "You wearing that?"

I double check the fitted Gap jeans and cropped T-shirt that Mama says must be from Baby Gap it's so short.

"I mean, yeah." I angle a defiant look up at him. "What's wrong with it?"

"It's slutty, and I don't want my boys checking you out. We too close to the championship for me to be kicking a teammate's ass."

"It's not slutty. Boys get on my nerves expecting us to dress like nuns because they get hard every time we wear clothes that show our shape. If your boys are disciplined enough to be in that weight room at the crack of dawn and practice every day, they should be able to see a little bit of ass fully covered by jeans without getting it up. And if they can't? Not my problem."

"I'm just saying I don't want them getting no ideas." His scowl deepens. "And I don't want you getting any either."

"Don't worry 'bout that. Your teammates are the boyest boys I ever met. I know them all except that new guy."

"Don't get any ideas about the new guy. Not that he's that new. He's been on the team all season."

"He ain't been to the house."

"He's kind of a loner."

"Maybe he just doesn't like you," I offer sweetly.

He turns to the mirror and checks out my handiwork with the tie. "Everybody likes me."

Arrogant, but accurate. The boy's charisma rivals his jump shot. Which makes him charming to everyone, but sometimes unbearable to his younger sister.

"What kind of name is Naz?" I ask. "Like Nas the rapper?"

"Pronounced the same, but short for Nazareth. Who names their kid that?"

"His mama, I guess," I laugh, leaning against the dresser and watching as Cliff removes his wave cap and brushes his hair. "I think it's kind of sexy."

"Tee, what'd I say?" Cliff shoots me a glare. "Stay away from my teammates—especially that one. He's gunning for my spot."

"Your spot? He's a two-guard?"

"He plays the two or the three. He's my backup, but Coach Lipton ain't taking my ass out 'less he has to. Got good old Naz riding that bench," he says with obvious satisfaction. "Scrub ass."

"Sounds like you got beef with him."

"Nah. Long as he stays in his place."

"Which is where?"

"Outta my way and on that bench."

"Well, you're the star," I say dryly. "Everyone stays out of your way, right?"

He narrows his eyes, brows lowering. "You being sarcastic?"

"No. Derisive. See the big words my basic public school education taught me?"

He huffs out a laugh and hooks an elbow around my neck, pulling me in close. "You'll be at the championship game, right? It's beat up you didn't make at least one game this season."

"Excuse me for having a life," I say, my brows peaking at his nerve and self-centeredness.

"What you doing that's so important you missed my games?"

I pull back to peer up at his handsome face. "Do you really not know I'm working at Ms. Hattie's shop every day after school?"

"Doing what?"

"Whatever she tells me to do. Sweeping. Washing and drying towels." I beam with pride. "I just started shampooing."

"You still thinking about skipping college to do hair?" he asks, grabbing his school uniform blazer from the back of his desk chair.

"I'm thinking about going to community college *to do* hair. I need training. Just because it's not a four-year degree doesn't mean it's not what's right for me. You're planning to skip college to ball in the league as soon as you can, right?" I wait for the nod I know is coming. "What's the difference? We both know what we want and see the path to get us there."

"Well, I'm guaranteed one and done. I'll be drafted after my freshman year." He slips Air Force Ones onto his feet. "I just don't want you to settle and be stuck here all your life."

"What's wrong with Houston?"

"Nothing, I guess. It's just where we grew up. What we've always known. If I had to stay here forever, not see anything else, not *be* anything else, I'd suffocate. It's the dream of getting out that keeps me motivated."

"What if you get drafted by Houston and your butt ends up staying right here after all?"

"If I'm playing ball, even here ain't *here*. I'll be at a different place in life. Traveling all over the country, all over the world. Nothing but money and opportunity. You think I'm being scouted now? Wait'll we win the big game." His mouth hardens. "So Naz can forget playing time. I need every minute on the floor I can get."

"Well, I'm sure you have nothing to worry about. You the best, right?"

"Damn right." The irritation clears from his expression. "You know wherever I end up, there's a place for you with me."

"What? With your groupies? No, thank you."

"I'm serious, Tee." He pulls me in for a side hug. "If I'm good, you good. I mean that. I'mma always make sure you straight."

"I know." I loop an arm around his waist. "You may be a pain in the ass."

"Excuse me?" he asks, pulling back to glare/grin down at me.

"But you're my pain in the ass," I finish, giving him one final squeeze.

"Kira!" Mama's voice booms from downstairs. "Cliff! Get down here. Somebody just pulled into the driveway."

"Here we go," he mutters, heading out the door and down the stairs.

A steady stream of towering boys invades our house over the next twenty minutes. Mama may have grumbled when Cliff first asked if he could host a pre-championship party at the house, but she's in her element, surrounded by hungry people. Her smooth brown skin shines with a light sheen of perspiration from living in that kitchen all day. The more people who crowd into our house, the wider her smile grows.

"I know we're still getting our plates," Cliff says, standing at the mantle over the fireplace, "but I wanted to say a few things before we get lost in my mama's food. Y'all thank her for a taste of the West Indies."

All the boys whoop and holler, some pretending to bow to her.

"Awww, thank you, sweet boys," Mama says. "But it wasn't just me. Takira helped."

I feel the weight of all eyes on me, and I smile stiffly, sliding my hands into the back pockets of my jeans. A few of the guys sneak glances at my bare midriff and down the length of my legs. It makes me want to cover myself, to hide myself, but I stand still despite the discomfort.

Like I said. The boyest boys.

"Yeah, thank you to my *baby* sister," Cliff says, slipping a little steel into the mild words to warn them off. I'm surprised he didn't douse me with a pesticide to keep them away.

Myron, one of Cliff's first friends at St. Catherine's, offers a mocking salute. "We hear you loud and clear, Cap. Hands off."

My cheeks heat, and I shuffle my feet uncomfortably. Passing around plates, Mama pauses long enough to glare like she might take her shoe off and throw it at anybody she catches looking too hard at me.

"You got that right," Cliff says, looking each of his teammates in the eyes. "But we're not here to talk about how I'll break your hand if you even think about it."

He pauses for the nervous laughter before going on. "We're here to celebrate the best season St. Catherine's has ever had," he says. "And party like that trophy is already ours."

They whoop and high five, which to my thinking is premature since that trophy *isn't* actually theirs yet. Cliff walks through life with this sense of inevitability, like his success is only a matter of time. I try to forecast everything that could go wrong, whereas Cliff seems to expect that nothing—at least for him—ever will.

When the doorbell rings, Mama, who just sat down, rises from her recliner in the corner.

"I got it, Mama," I say, shooing her back down. She's been on her feet all day.

"Probably Coach," Myron says. "He's supposed to be stopping through, even though he can't stay."

I walk to the foyer and pull the door open.

And the world stops.

My breath can't quite seem to make the trip from my lungs to my mouth. My heart pounds against my rib cage like a tassa drum as I stare up and up at the most beautiful boy I've ever seen in real life. Dark brown skin stretches over the chiseled planes of his face. I've never actually seen anyone with a square chin, but he has one. Everything seems to be at odds on his face. His nose is too bold. His lips too full and soft looking. His brows too heavy and severe. His eyes, warm and dark like velvet, framed by a feathering of sooty lashes. But somehow, all those disparate parts cooperate into a face so striking, my jaw falls open.

"Um..." His voice is a low, quiet rumble as he peers over my shoulder into the foyer. "Is this Cliff's house? I took a wrong turn, but..."

Just as I'm about to shake myself out of the stupor, I stop because, all of a sudden, it feels like the same rapt way I was watching him, he's now studying me. I go still as if with his eyes, he's painting me, and I don't want to distract him.

"Who's at the door, Kira?" Mama asks from behind, drawing up beside me. "Oh, hey, Nazareth."

Wait. Nazareth as in…Naz?

She extends her arms, and with a smile, he crosses the threshold and walks into them, bending to return her squeeze.

"Mrs. Fletcher." He pulls back and offers her a bouquet of wildflowers I hadn't noticed. Who cares about flowers when you've got *this* guy standing in front of you? "These are for you."

"Hmmm. Thank you." Mama buries her nose in the flowers and smiles up at Naz. "And how's your mama doing? Didn't she have surgery on her knee a while back?"

His expression clouds, and he nods. "Yes, ma'am. She just went back to work."

"She teaches, right?" Mama asks.

"Seventh grade, yeah." His eyes flick from Mama, settle on me briefly, and then shift back to Mama. "I guess the team's already here? Sorry I'm late."

"You right on time." Mama links her arm through his and guides him toward the living room and the increasingly rowdy basketball team. "Come on. We're about to start eating."

I haven't moved, my feet sealed to the floor like I've stepped into fast-drying cement. He glances back over his shoulder. Our eyes catch and hold, some odd understanding passing between us. Whatever that jolt was when I first saw him, I think he felt it, too. I *know* it, but I don't know what to do with it. How could I when nothing like this has ever happened to me before?

I take a minute to collect my scattered thoughts before heading back into the living room. Everyone's eating, plates balanced on their knees or on the big table in the middle of the room. Mama, making sure everyone has drinks, looks up when I return.

"Go check on Naz in the kitchen," she says. "Make sure he doesn't need anything."

My pulse quickens at the thought of me and that beautiful boy alone. "Yes, ma'am."

When I enter the kitchen, sure enough, Naz is staring at all the dishes, his empty plate held between two huge hands.

"Need help?" I ask, walking farther into the kitchen to lean against the counter.

"Uh, maybe." He points to a few covered dishes. "Is any of that fish? I don't really eat chicken or beef."

"What about duck?" I ask, nodding to a plate of curried duck.

His nose scrunches. "No, and not any goat either."

"Oh, well, goat is all we have left."

He looks at me like he's not sure if I'm joking.

"If my granny was here, you'd be eating goat tonight. You don't turn that woman down." I laugh and lift the lid on the soup. "How about fish soup and a few vegetables and coconut bread. Sound good?"

"Perfect. I don't wanna be difficult."

"Difficult?" I scoff. "Cliff makes me crack his crab legs and dig out all the meat. He's the resident diva."

Naz laughs and raises his brows but doesn't reply. I take his plate and start loading it with the dishes I know only contain vegetables and seafood.

"I've never had food from Trinidad," he says, considering the abundance of dishes spread across the stove and counters.

"Then you been missing out. We may live in Houston, but we Trini through and through."

"I see." He nods to the scroll hanging on the wall by the fridge. "What's that about?"

"Oh, you gonna find one of those in just about every Trinidad-American household."

"Trinidad and Tobago, Land of Calypso," he reads, stepping closer to inspect the souvenir scroll depicting our islands, population, exports. Even the limbo dance and national bird are pictured there.

"We never forget where we come from," I say, repeating something my father has said all our lives.

His eyes shift from the wall scroll to study my face. "I really appreciate your family sharing your food and culture with us like this."

"It's nothing," I say with a shrug, though it's everything to us. There's no greater pride than Trini pride.

"So why haven't we seen you around this season?" he asks, eyes following my hands drifting between dishes and heaping food on his plate. "Your mom's been at just about every game."

"I have a job after school, so I don't have many free nights."

"What do you do?"

"I work at a hair salon," I say, facing the stove to serve up some of the fish soup. "I want to be a stylist."

"You're what? A junior?"

"Actually, a senior." I turn and hand him the plate. "Cliff had a late birthday and I had an early one, so we ended up starting school together.

We're really close in age. Mama and Daddy didn't waste no time having us kids."

His chuckle is a deep, husky thing that makes me shiver. I fix my eyes to the tile floor, afraid that if I look, I'll stare. There is just something about this guy. It's deeper than his good looks and gorgeous body. He seems to be around the same height as Cliff, but broader and leaner. It feels like his arms and legs are still trying to catch up with how his body grew so big so fast. It lends him a ranginess, an almost physical uncertainty Cliff shed years ago.

Silence stretches between us to the point of awkwardness, so I hazard a glance up at him only to find him staring at me. Uncomfortable, I slide my eyes to the side, away from the intensity of that look. Of the way it heats me up inside until it feels like my heart may melt and puddle at my feet.

He clears his throat. "Sorry."

My eyes snap to his. "For what?"

"For staring." A rueful grin crooks his full lips. "No wonder Fletcher warned us to stay away from his sister."

I suck my teeth, huffing out an irritated breath. "That boy works my nerves."

"He was just looking out for you. He knows how guys are and wanted us to know the shit some of them try with other girls, they better not try with you. Protective big brother. I have three sisters. I get it."

A roar of laughter from the living room cuts into our conversation. He turns his head toward the sound almost reluctantly. "I guess I better get in there."

"Right." I grab one of the red cups on the counter already filled with ice. "Lemme get you something to drink. Soda? Tea? Lemonade?"

"Water?"

I grab a bottle of water and hand it to him. Our fingers brush, and that shiver returns, shimmying down my spine. A slow smile inches onto his mouth, and he looks from where our fingers touch to my face.

"You should go," I say in a rush. "You're missing everything."

"No, I'm not."

The air throbs between us like a pulse, and we hold each other's gaze hostage. In the living room, the team claps for something, and it snaps the thread between our eyes, freeing me to look away.

"I better..." He points his thumb over his shoulder and leaves the kitchen.

I slump against the counter, my breath coming out in a stream of forced air. What the heck? I've had boyfriends. Kissed guys. Gone all the way a few times. Nothing to write home about. If anything, I made it out to be more than it was when I told my friends because…surely there was supposed to be *more*? More than fumbling hands and squishy lips and boozy breath and a guy getting his, but never thinking about mine. Besides not getting me off—which I can do in my bed by myself—those guys didn't touch me. Not with their clumsy, seeking hands, but in my heart. Shoot, in my soul. They were so worried about touching all the parts they got to see, they didn't bother with the parts invisible to the naked eye. Those parts— *the under the skin, stirring in my chest, burning up my heart parts*—Naz somehow seemed to touch in a matter of glances, with a few words and a simple brush of my fingers.

"You been watching too much *Vampire Diaries*," I mutter, laughing at my own whimsical thoughts.

I know that's television, fantasy, fiction, but if love ain't epic, I don't want it. If it ain't life and death—not literally, the way it is for Stefan, Damon, and Elena—but if it's not something that makes you risk, makes you ache, then why bother?

I'm scarfing down some coconut bread when the guys start bringing their paper plates into the kitchen and tossing them in the trash.

"You guys ready to take pictures?" Cliff asks. "For posterity, I think is what they call it. The night before we shook up the world."

"Wow," I mutter, tying off a bag of trash. "It's a ball game, not a revolution."

"Don't let them hear you say that."

I glance up to find Naz standing beside me.

"Oh. I just meant…well." My words tangle up. "Just meant that, um, you guys think the whole world revolves around that court."

"I don't." He shrugs. "But it may be my best shot at a full ride for college, so it's important, yeah."

"How good are you?" I tease, smiling and leaning against the edge of the sink.

"Not as good as your brother, but who is?"

"Strongarm," Cliff calls from the kitchen door, his glance pinging suspiciously between Naz and me. "We're going up on the roof for pictures. Come on."

"On the roof?" Naz frowns.

"My daddy made it a rooftop we could use for cookouts and stuff. It's actually kind of cool."

"And totally safe," Mama says, entering just behind Cliff.

"Mama, can you come take some pictures of us?" Cliff asks.

"Get your sister to do it." Mama shakes her head. "I spent my whole day cooking all that food for you. Don't ask me for another thing."

Cliff rolls his eyes up to the ceiling and releases a long-suffering sigh. "Will you do it, Tee?"

"Um, yeah." I make sure not to look at Naz so Cliff won't kick him out.

By the time we've climbed the steps to reach the roof, the guys are lined up in their sports jackets and ties. They're all laughing. That same sense of invincibility Cliff carries—he's managed to imbue his team with it. They're all so boisterous and cocksure, except Naz. It's obvious to me these guys have been together for three years, and that Naz is still trying to find his place. Even in the photos, there's something that sets him apart, makes him seem alone even in the midst of boys dressed exactly the same.

I use Daddy's camera and also take a few with my phone. After thirty minutes of them posing and me snapping, I stop.

"Cliff, I have enough pics for three championships," I say. "We done?"

"Yeah, yeah." He comes over and squeezes my shoulders, bending to kiss my forehead. "Thanks, Tee."

He turns to his team and lifts his arms, releasing a shout. "That's a wrap. Now take your ugly asses home and get some sleep. Tomorrow will be here before you know it."

I hang back, waiting for the roof to clear. When the last of their shrieks dies out, I grab the blanket from a storage bench, spread it on the cement floor, and sit. Between my parents and siblings, and all of Cliff's friends who are always at the house, it can get pretty crowded. It can be hard to think in all the noise. It can become impossible to dream, so I come up here every chance I get to be alone.

"Thanks again for taking the pictures."

I turn, smiling when I see Naz standing at the top of the stairs leading back into the house. He walks over to the wall where the team posed minutes ago.

"Forgot this," he says, grabbing his uniform jacket.

"No 'fabulous' on your tie?" I ask. Immediately, I regret the comment. Cliff said it was just for starters. Naz might be sensitive about riding the bench.

"Not for backups." He smiles, watching me stretched out on the blanket. I resist the temptation to fold my arms over my bare stomach. His eyes are on my face anyway, and he doesn't creep me out like some of

Cliff's other friends do.

"Well." He holds up the jacket. "Guess I better go."

"What's your name?" I blurt, sitting up on the blanket. It's the first thing that came to mind that might keep him here a few minutes longer. I take a deep breath of the cooling night air, hoping to calm how crazily my heart is beating.

He freezes, turns, and walks over to where I sit on the blanket.

"You know my name," he says, sliding his hands into his pockets. "It's Nazareth. Naz."

"Yeah, but some of the guys called you Armstrong and some said Strongarm." I slant a curious glance up at him. "Which is it?"

"That's kind of a long story." That mouth God took extra time with pushes into a one-sided grin.

"Your *name* is a long story?"

"Well, the story behind why it's both kind of is."

Knowing Cliff will kill me first and then kill Naz for what I'm about to do, I pat the blanket beside me anyway. "I got a few minutes."

Then

Naz

I shouldn't.

Fletcher has been very clear, on more than one occasion with more than one guy on the team, that his sister is off-limits. Now I know why.

She glows.

In a world that feels gray, she's a burst of color, and she shines. Her smile makes a face that is already pretty gorgeous. Her skin is richly brown and luminous. Two neat braids hang on her shoulders.

I glance toward the stairs that lead back into the house, but I already know I'll accept Takira's invitation. I do recognize her question for what it is—an excuse for me to stay. Any other girl tried this, I'd run in the other direction. Though I'm not the biggest star on the team, there's something about me that attracts girls *now*. It wasn't always this way. I was the quiet, nerdy guy reading comic books on the bus until seventh grade. My body took over—started filling out and growing up—fast. It got me noticed in ways I'd never been noticed before. I'm still not completely used to this body or the attention it brings.

"Never mind." Takira looks down at her hands resting on the long legs crisscrossed beneath her on the blanket. "Sorry. I know you have a game tomorrow."

Wordlessly, I take the spot beside her, laying the jacket between us.

She gives me a tentative smile and draws her knees up to her chest, wrapping her arms around them.

"My last name is Armstrong," I tell her. "But in middle school, I started playing football. I got really good. I was a quarterback. Everybody said I had such a good toss, people started calling me Strongarm instead of

Armstrong. Even though I play basketball now, it kinda stuck."

"So if you were good at football, why come play a sport you're not as good at?"

I huff out a surprised laugh.

"Sorry," she rushes to say, lowering her knees and turning to face me. "I just meant...well—"

"No, you're right. I was better at football, but..." I gesture toward the long stretch of my legs on the blanket. "Growth spurt, sophomore year. There are exceptions, but most quarterbacks aren't six foot seven."

"You couldn't play football anymore?" she asks, frowning.

"Probably. Let's just say recruiters weren't banging down the door for a guy built like me as their quarterback. I mean, I could probably try some other position, but I always played basketball, too. Both coaches, basketball and football, sat me down and said if I really wanted a shot at the pros for either sport, I might want to choose."

"And you chose basketball."

"Basketball kind of chose me." I shake my head, still unsure how I got here sometimes. "Coach Lipton saw me play and recruited me to St. Catherine's."

"He recruited Cliff, too. Mama said there was no way Cliff wasn't going. Free prep school education, not to mention their reputation for players going division one."

"Yeah. It's hard to turn down." I hesitate but go on, for some reason willing to share with this girl what I haven't shared with many people. "My, um, mom's got some health issues. Really bad arthritis and it's getting worse. I want to see her retire early if she can. Get her medical bills paid. Maybe buy her a house someday. Make sure my three sisters are set up."

I laugh self-deprecatingly and say, "Stereotype, huh? Baller makes it out the 'hood. Gets a fat contract. Takes care of his mama."

"You live in the 'hood?"

"Nope. The 'burbs."

We laugh together at that.

"What about your dad?" she asks.

"Died when I was in fifth grade."

"I'm sorry." Her brows bunch up, and her dark eyes hold a world of sympathy.

"Yeah, it was unexpected. Stroke. He was young, but..." I shrug. "Took him out, and even though two of my sisters are older than me, I felt like the man of the house, ya know? Like I'm supposed to take care of them or whatever."

I look down at my hands, unused to talking this much but finding it too easy to stop.

"I love basketball, but not the way Cliff and some of the guys do. It's a means to an end. I don't breathe ball like your brother."

"No one does," she says dryly. "Ball has been his whole life for as long as I can remember."

"So why hair?" I ask, changing the subject because we probably don't have much time. Who wants to talk about her brother when I could be learning more about *her?*

"Why not hair? I like to make people look good. It makes *me* feel good seeing how just getting her hair done can boost a woman's confidence. Maybe one day I can be in the thick of things. New York City. Hollywood. Making famous people beautiful. Regular folks, too." She laughs. "You gotta start somewhere."

It's getting dark now with only the moon and a few fairy lights strung on the roof for illumination. The darkness softens the lines of her body, but I can see her turn her head and look at me—sense her searching my face in the dim light.

"You think you'll get some looks from colleges?" she asks.

"Playing backup for the best baller in the city?" I chuckle, leaning back on my elbows. "Probably not. My old coach offered to put some feelers out to a few football programs. I may not make it to the NFL, but I got good tape. Even if I just win a scholarship, play for four years, get a business degree—that's better than nothing. I'd actually be pretty happy with that."

"A backup with a backup plan," she teases.

"I guess. I'm not Cliff. I need options if I expect to succeed."

"You're not like Cliff, no," she says. "But that doesn't mean you don't have ambition. Things you want. They're just not all about you."

I nod slowly because she's right. I *am* ambitious. The need to help my mom, to provide for my family and set up their futures—it burns in me.

"I'll do whatever it takes to help my family," I say. "If I thought digging ditches was the best way to make that happen, I'd grab a shovel. If it's not ball, it'll be something else."

She giggles at that, and it draws a smile from me, too.

"I know Cliff would have nothing without ball, but that's not me." I shoot her a sharp glance. The guy may be an asshole eighty-five percent of the time, but he *is* her brother. "Sorry. I didn't mean—"

"No, you're right. He probably would shrivel up without ball. He can't imagine a life where *this* dream doesn't come true." She tips her head back and stares up at the sky. "I just hope it does."

The smooth line of her neck is exposed, and her breasts rise and fall with easy breaths under the shirt cropped at her belly button.

"Are you checking me out?" she asks, flipping onto her side and propping her head in her palm. "Because guys have drawn back a nub for less."

"You're very pretty," I say softly, finding it hard to joke about the effect she's having on me. "I like you a lot."

Shit. Why'd I say that?

I'm not good with girls. Like, yeah, they come to me because I'm an athlete and they want to say they've been with a guy from the team, but that doesn't mean I'm that dude who says the right things or knows how to flirt.

Instead of responding to my awkward statement, she stares back at me, blinking long lashes before turning onto her back.

"Look how bright the stars are tonight," she says, biting her bottom lip and watching me from the corner of her eye.

I ease down on the blanket beside her, careful not to let any of our body parts touch. I fold my hand under my head and consider the sky.

"Up here," I say, "they feel really close and bright."

"It's the quarter moon. Less moon, brighter stars. When there's a lot of moonlight, it hides them. Dims them."

Over the next hour or so, the noise below grows thinner as cars pull off and the guys leave. I keep holding my breath and stealing glances at the stairs, like someone will come up here any minute and make us stop, but no one comes, and we keep talking. She has this way of looking at the world that feels a lot like mine. She's filled with subtle ambition, too. Her brother's ambition blares in every room he enters, like a trumpet. Her hopes and dreams are quieter, but no less sure. I want to see where this girl will go because I think it will be far. Probably beyond my reach. I may only have these moments to know her.

It's a strange night. It feels out of time, like we've known each other for a century or more and the rhythm of the conversation is something we're resuming, not just beginning. Not something that will end. As it gets chilly, she pulls the corner of the blanket up over her legs, and I do the same. We're rolled up, and it pushes us closer together.

"We're an egg roll." She giggles.

I love her laugh. Low and breathy or when she's surprised into it, big, chasing away reservations. She gives her whole self to it, throwing back her head and once even slapping her knee. I wish I was funnier and had made her laugh more tonight. I don't have *lines*. I enjoy a good conversation—the kind that makes you think about who you are and get to know someone else. The kind that makes you laugh at yourself and want to make someone else laugh over and over because in just a few hours, you've grown addicted to the sound.

I glance at my watch and swallow a curse.

"It's later than I thought. Coach'll kill me if I'm not ready tomorrow. Even though I'll probably ride the bench all night. Cliff's gonna play every minute he can with all those scouts at the game there to see him, but I gotta be ready."

"I hope you get some time to play, too." She frowns. "It's the last game of the season. It's not fair if you don't get *some* time on the court."

"It doesn't work like that. Besides, like I said, I may still get some looks for football."

"I hope so." She hesitates, bites down on her bottom lip before rushing on. "Maybe you could call me sometime, or..." She shakes her head and blows out a quick breath. "You don't have to. It's not like—"

"I will call you," I cut in. "I don't know where things are headed after this year, but we could stay in touch."

She beams, and that smile outshines the moon and the stars. "Yeah, I'd like that too."

I can't leave without...something. I want to touch her, to kiss her, but that might be weird. I'm still trying to figure out what move I should make when she makes it for me. She leans over and kisses my cheek. It's a friendly gesture, but as soon as her mouth touches my skin, the small flicker of heat that has simmered inside ever since I laid eyes on her in that tiny top and those tight jeans roars to full flame. I turn my head, kissing the corner of her mouth. She stills, her wide eyes searching my face. Without looking away, her tongue darts out to lick my bottom lip. I groan, cupping her head in my hand, dipping to suck her bottom lip and then the top. She pushes closer under the blanket, pressing into my chest, straining up to open my lips with hers.

"Takira," I whisper, sharing a breath with her. "We should stop."

"No." She shakes her head, kissing my chin and touching my cheekbone. "Kiss me again."

I can't resist her, especially not when the lust, the desire I've been feeling for her all night is so clearly reciprocated in her eyes, in the way she touches me. I kiss the fragile line of her collarbone and suck at the satiny, sweet-smelling skin of her throat. My lips coast up to the small cleft in her chin. I notch my tongue into that little indentation, and she laughs, shifting her head to kiss me again.

This time it's deeper, hotter. My hands wander down to her ass. It looked so good in these jeans, but in my hands—God, my dick is so hard. She touches me through my jeans, and I pull away from the kiss to draw in a deep breath.

"Takira," I pant. "Don't do that. I won't be able to…I want to…"

She places my hand on her chest, looking at me and not breaking the stare. Her breast is soft and spills over the edges of my hand. I squeeze, and she moans, her eyes drifting closed as she leans deeper into my palm. I brush my finger across the nipple, and it goes hard.

"That feels good," she gasps. "Keep doing it."

With one hand, I knead her breast. The other hand wanders down her back, palming her ass, cupping her hip. Turned on her side, she opens her legs, resting her knee on my thigh and biting my earlobe, then soothing, sucking it into her mouth.

"You can touch me," she whispers, guiding my hand between her legs.

Even through the denim, I can feel that she's hot there.

"You sure?" I ask, frowning. "We don't have to."

"I want you to, Naz."

Searching her face, I nod and slowly lower her zipper. The sound is loud on the roof, and I glance up at the stars as if they might judge me, might stop me from taking something I desire this much. When my fingers slip into her jeans, past the edge of her cotton panties and to the slit of her pussy, she gasps, breath leaving her in a whoosh.

"Oh, my god," she says, panting as I slide my finger over her clit, repeating the motion until her hips are moving in time with my touch. She rolls onto her back and eases her jeans and panties down, spreading her legs.

I shove her shirt up, squeezing her breast through the bra. Her nipples pebble beneath the fabric, and I bend down, nudging the satin cup away and taking her nipple into my mouth.

"Naz," she moans.

"You have great tits, Kira," I manage to say. "You're beautiful."

I cup her pussy and slip a finger inside. She's so tight, and the slick walls clamp around my finger like a fist. I don't want to assume or hurt her.

"Are you a…" I press my lips closed over whatever awkward thing I was about to say. "Have you ever—"

"I'm not a virgin, Naz. It's okay."

I keep rubbing her clit. It's swollen, and she's so wet and tight. I ease in another finger, watching her expression for clues that it feels good or if it hurts.

"Yes." Her eyes roll back. "Naz. Don't stop."

"Kira," I groan, taking her breast into my mouth, licking the darker halo of skin around her nipple. As my fingers move in and out of her tightness, I can't help but imagine how it will feel when that's me. When she's spread under me and I can push into her. Wetness seeps into my briefs. I'm leaking at the thought. Her eyes squeeze shut, and she bites her lip. She grips my wrist, and her back arches, a cry trapped in her throat as she soaks my hand.

"Did you just…" I falter, not sure. "Did you just come?"

She nods jerkily. "No one's ever made me come before. Only when I touched myself. *That's* what they were talking about?"

Laughing, the sound rich and delighted and floating in the crisp air, she turns on her side to face me. Her kiss-swollen lips pull into a wide smile. Reaching between us, she grabs my dick through my jeans and says, "Your turn."

"Takira!" Cliff's voice climbs the stairs. "You up here? Mama's looking for you."

"Oh, shit!" she whisper-shouts, moving swiftly beneath the blanket to pull up her underwear and jeans. "He'll kill you."

"Fuck!"

We scramble to our feet, and she shoves the blanket into a storage bench. Her hair is all over the place, one of her braids halfway unraveled. I can clearly see that one cup of her bra is still pulled down beneath her shirt, and her hard nipple pushes against the thin fabric. Her jeans are pulled up and zipped, but unbuttoned. Cliff's heavy footsteps echo up to us, and my heart triple times in my chest, but I take a second to pull her toward me so I can fix her clothes.

"You're a mess," I mutter, buttoning her jeans and reaching beneath her shirt to pull her bra into place. I have no idea how to braid, but I'm trying to smooth her hair when our eyes catch.

Damn, she's pretty.

There's something luminescent about her skin, and her lips are rosy, like all the blood has rushed to them. Her eyes—her eyes outshine the stars, and I'm gone. My heart melts in my chest looking at her. She grins up at me and laughs, shaking her head. It's no use pretending, and I don't care what her brother thinks.

"What the hell are you doing up here with my sister, Armstrong?" Cliff growls at the door leading to the rooftop. He looks at where my hand rests at her waist, at the smooth skin bared by her shirt. "I'm gonna kick your ass."

"No, you're not." Takira steps in front of me. "Cliff, stop."

"I got this," I whisper in her ear. "Let me—"

"We're just talking," she says. "I stayed up here after the team left. You know how I like it up here. Naz forgot his jacket, came back to get it, and we started talking."

"Everyone else left two hours ago," Cliff snaps, narrowed eyes sending me kill messages. "You been up here *talking* that long?"

"I know your conversations consist of grunts, half-formed thoughts, and plays from a handbook," Takira says, her tone dry, "but some people do talk. Unlike most of your teammates, Naz can actually hold a conversation."

Cliff looks at me suspiciously, and with good reason. My jacket covers a monster erection that probably won't go down for days.

"Well, the game is tomorrow," Cliff finally says, his tone still rough, but his breathing more even. "Go home and get ready to ride that bench, scrub."

Resentment rises in me—that because of him I never get to play, that he holds it over my head all the time and tries to demean me in front of the team because of his own insecurities. Most of all, I resent that because of him, I have to leave Takira.

We're all walking down the steps from the roof when she catches a fistful of my T-shirt at my back. A step above and behind me, she bends to whisper in my ear, "Tomorrow. After the game?"

I turn my head and meet the velvety brown of her eyes and nod. I'll ride the bench tomorrow, and no one will see what I'm capable of. I'll have to figure out what I'm doing for college. I've accepted that, but what I won't accept is not seeing Takira again.

"Yeah," I say, smiling back at her. "After the game."

Chapter One
Takira

Twelve Years Later

"So what do you do?" the man seated across from me asks.

You mean besides meet random people online over and over on Groundhog dates, only to be disappointed time and time again?

"Um," I say aloud instead. "I do hair and makeup."

"Ahhhh," Calvin—if that's even his real name—says. "Right. That *was* on your profile. Like in a salon or something?"

"Mostly in entertainment. Film, television, photo shoots. Stuff like that."

"Oh." Calvin's brows lift as if I've impressed him. "Any stuff I'd know?"

"Well, I just wrapped on that new Canon Holt biopic, *Dessi Blue*. Have you heard of it?"

"Wow. Yeah." If possible, Calvin's brows climb even higher but then dip into a disapproving V over his eyes. "You must be pretty successful, huh?"

Oh, Lord. One of them?

If they aren't sleeping on your couch and asking for gas money, they're pissed off and intimidated that you earn more than they do. *Or* they're so obsessed with making money they barely have time to take you out and get you off before the night is over. I swear, the last guy may as well have had one hand on his phone and one between my legs with the little bit of attention he paid me. How do you get lost down there? And yet, a surprising number of men seem unable to find their way around a clit these days.

"I do all right," I say warily, casting a longing glance toward the door leading to the street. "What about you? Your profile said you're an artist. That's exciting. Would I see your art anywhere? Shows? Exhibits?"

"I mostly do drawings at events. Kids' birthday parties, bar mitzvahs— stuff like that," he says, the look he offers a little sheepish. "I didn't think that sounded as good so I may have flubbed a little on my profile."

Flubbed a little?

The only apparent similarities between Calvin and his dating app profile is that he is actually a man. When I entered the restaurant, I walked right past him, not realizing the guy standing by the door who was maybe an inch shorter than I am was supposed to be the six-foot-four Adonis from the profile pic.

"Drawing is really...cool," I murmur, picking up my menu and immediately going straight for the drinks like a heat-seeking missile. "Should we order?"

An hour later, I can *feel* my brain mushing. I wouldn't be surprised if my soul is oozing from my ears. If this date is a preview of hell, I'm running up the aisle and falling on the altar this Sunday. Begging God to hear my cry. It's not because this man ekes out his living drawing children at parties. At least he's gainfully employed, which is more than I can say for Bart from Hinge. It's not because he tells the server it will be separate checks as soon as she takes our drink order. Gary from Match didn't even bother bringing his wallet. Calvin's dull, sure, but Ginger from Plenty of Fish regaled me about the wonders of her work as a shoe fitter the entire date.

The problem is I'm completely unmoved by Calvin. Not a flutter in my belly. Not a pussy twitch. Not a quickening pulse. My heart may as well be a lump of clay in my chest. I'm so tired of going on these dates *hoping* to feel something and feeling absolutely nothing.

I'm considering another drink when the phone in my purse rings.

"You need to get that?" Calvin asks.

"Oh!" My hands practically shake fumbling to reach my bag, my lifeline. "Yeah, I do."

I didn't ask anyone to do the ol' *call to interrupt a bad date* trick, but this is evidence that God must still be on my side. I barely even glance at the screen before I answer. I'd talk to a scammer right now to get out of here.

"Hello," I say breathlessly, feigning an apologetic look to Calvin.

"Hey, boo," my best friend Neevah booms from the other line. "What you doing?"

"I'm on a...a date," I lend weight to the word because Neevah is the one who endures my belly aching every time a date crashes and burns.

"Oh, shit. What should I have?" Neevah whispers. "Appendicitis? Broken bone? I'm too superstitious to fake a death in the family."

"It's fine," I say, keeping my tone even and flashing a reassuring smile at Calvin. "What's going on?"

"You know Lotus Ross?" Neevah asks. "The fashion designer?"

"Of course." My heartbeat kicks up, thumping harder than it has the last hour in Calvin's company.

"She has a celebrity fashion show tomorrow, and one of her stylists can't make it. You remember Catalina, who came on set that time? Has her own wig line?"

"Oh, yeah. She was cool."

"She's coordinating the show and called asking if maybe you could step in."

"Girl, yes. You know it." Lotus is a rising star in the fashion world, has one of the hottest lines out there, gLO, and recently opened her flagship store in downtown LA.

"Good! I'll text you deets for tomorrow."

"All right. Bet."

As soon as we disconnect, I school my expression to one of distress and turn concerned eyes to Calvin. "I have an emergency and need to go."

I lift my hand, signaling for the server to bring the bill.

"That's a shame." Calvin's face falls. "What is it?"

"Huh?" I ask distractedly, smiling at the server as she drops my half of the bill on the table.

"The emergency," he reminds me with a small frown.

"Oh." My mind scrabbles for the emergency that is springing me from this hellish date. "Appendicitis."

God, forgive me.

Chapter Two
Takira

There's nothing like a show.

I've done hair and makeup for theater, TV, film, commercials, award shows. You name it. Over the last twelve years, I've done it. The excitement of preparing someone to shine never gets old. It infiltrates the air as I venture backstage for Lotus Ross's celebrity fashion show. I accepted the opportunity blindly, so eager to work with Lotus in any capacity. I didn't even ask which charity the show was benefiting, but in the hotel lobby, I passed a sign for Harbor House, which I believe focuses on domestic violence, a cause I know is close to her cousin Iris's heart, and consequently, to Lotus's, too.

Makeshift stations are set up backstage with small mirrors and chairs. Stylists heft bags stuffed with makeup and tools of the beauty trade. It's been a while since I worked a fashion show, celebrity or otherwise, and I'd forgotten how tall everyone is. I'm five nine, so no small woman, but I'm dwarfed by the Amazons and giants milling around the area designated for hair and makeup.

"Takira!"

I turn my head in the direction of my name being called. An attractive woman with dark curly hair and golden-brown skin approaches, dressed in all black—T-shirt and jeans—like most of the other stylists here. Like me.

"Catalina, hey." I accept her quick hug and return her genuine smile. "Thanks for thinking of me."

"You were the first one I thought of," she says, her slight accent drawing out her vowels. If I remember correctly, she's from Colombia. "I saw the great work you did on set that day. And I liked you. In this town, it can be hard to find competence and kindness in the same package."

"You telling me." I chuckle in agreement.

I relocated from New York to LA for *Dessi Blue* when Neevah was cast as the lead and secured a position for me in the crew. Say what you want about New Yorkers being rude. With them, you get what you get and you know what it is. Here, there sometimes seems to be a thin layer of plastic laid over most interactions. In a place that makes its money off illusions, it's hard to know what and who is real.

"Lemme introduce you to Lo," Catalina says, glancing at her watch. "We got a lot of ground to cover before the show starts, and we're dealing with a bunch of amateurs today."

"I thought I saw some big-time models." I follow her, shifting the bag on my shoulder as we pick our way over the chaos on the floor and the racks of clothing parked throughout the space.

"Watch your step," she warns. "It's a mess back here. Yeah, some great models, for sure, but I'd say half the guys are ballers."

"You mean like—"

"Basketball players." Catalina shoots me a bright grin. "You know Lotus is married to Kenan Ross."

"He's retired, right?"

"Not too long ago, but he's still got a lot of friends on the San Diego Waves and all throughout the league. He called in some favors. Lotta folks want to see these guys strutting down the catwalk. Good for Harbor House."

When she says *San Diego Waves*, a kernel of unease takes root in my belly. I barely have time to consider why before we reach a petite woman on her knees with pins in her mouth, kneeling in front of a statuesque model whose dress she's tugging.

"Lo," Catalina says, bending a little to catch the popular designer's attention. "I want you to meet someone if you have a sec."

"Oh, sure." Lotus stretches a hand up to the model, who gently pulls until Lotus is standing to her full, if modest, height.

"You're pregnant!" I blurt, staring at her rounded belly.

"Looks that way." Lotus laughs, rubbing her stomach through the sheer, brightly patterned caftan that falls to her knees over wide-legged flowing pants and silk slippers. Small she may be, but there is something regal and commanding about her that draws the eye and refuses to let go.

"I'm sorry." I shake my head, feeling like an idiot. "Congratulations. I just didn't know."

"My husband Kenan is..." She rolls her eyes, tosses a swathe of platinum braids over her shoulder, and smiles. "Paranoid. We didn't tell anyone for a long time, and since I'm not the biggest chick to begin with, it was a while before I started showing. Anyway, yeah. Six months."

"And flyer than ever," Catalina purrs, side-hugging Lotus. "Lo, this is Takira, the makeup artist I told you about from *Dessi Blue*."

"I'm so excited for that movie," Lotus says, her eyes widening. "Please tell me it'll be out soon."

"Depends on what you mean by soon." I laugh. "We just wrapped, so I think they're editing and finalizing."

"I've heard Canon Holt is a genius." Lotus's eyes and nimble fingers stray back to the dress worn by the patiently waiting model. "And this new actress, Neevah. Heard great things about her, too."

"She's spectacular." I beam, unable to check my pride in my best friend.

"Takira may be slightly biased," Catalina chuckles, "since they're roommates."

"Former roommates," I correct.

"I did hear she and Canon are dating now," Lotus says, her eyes flicking from the collar of the dress she's pinning back to my face, speculation in her gaze. "What a gorgeous couple."

"Speaking of gorgeous couples," Catalina says. "Wanna show Takira all the handsome boys she gets to power today?"

"Oh, this is gonna be fun." Lotus nods at the model and sends her to a nearby makeup station. "Yours are all grumps whose arms I had to twist twice around to get them to do this show. Follow me."

Lotus walks ahead, her confident stride leading us through the maze of stations and bags.

"Some of these guys are former teammates of Kenan's," she tosses over her shoulder. "Some, just players from around the League. All of them have hearts of gold and really want to help raise money for Harbor House."

We walk quickly through the space, but I absorb as many details as I can. One particularly glamorous updo of bright pink hair turns my head, so I don't notice the overstuffed bag in my path. My feet slip from under me and there's no time to catch myself. Grappling with my own heavy bag, I yelp, halfway bracing for the inevitable fall…but it doesn't come. Instead I tumble into something hard, a wall of muscle and heat. Big arms enfold me, and I find myself pressed to a mountain of good-smelling man.

"I'm so sorry," I sputter, dragging my eyes from the wide expanse of white T-shirt stretched across a broad chest. "I…"

The rest of my apology slithers back down my throat, swallowed by a gasp of shock. I haven't seen the face above me in a long time—at least, not in person. The dark skin and carved bone structure is leaner and more pronounced now than it was before. Same square chin and bold nose and heavy brows. The guarded eyes are paradoxically framed by a feathering of long, curling lashes. He's still as arresting as he was the day I met him when I was eighteen years old, but I never thought I'd come face-to-face with him again.

"Takira," he says, the same surprise coloring his voice that I'm sure is scrawled all over my face.

I take a deep steadying breath that doesn't seem to be steadying anything before answering, "Naz."

Chapter Three

Naz

As soon as I agreed to do this fashion show, I regretted it. I even called Kenan, trying to get out of it.

"Sure," he had said. "You can pull out, but you have to tell Lo yourself. Oh, and tell Iris you don't actually care as much about survivors of domestic abuse as we originally assumed."

"Motherfucker," I'd muttered and hung up on his smart ass.

Needless to say, I'm here waiting to be powdered and brushed and groomed or some shit for charity, when something...*someone* soft and scented literally falls into my arms.

"What the hell?" I stumble a little but right myself before either of us fall and bust ass on the floor. I glance down to see who I've caught, and any words I would say cling to the roof of my mouth. I manage to pull one word down, despite my shock. Her name.

"Takira."

It's the first time I've seen her in twelve years. At least, in person. I may have lurked on her Instagram account and tracked her progress since senior year. On occasion.

"Naz." A sooty fan of lashes surrounds doe-brown eyes. Her chin bears the same tiny dent as her brother's. She's always been a smaller, softer, prettier version of Cliff Fletcher. Over the years, they've both haunted me for completely different reasons.

"You two know each other?" Lotus asks, her alert eyes pinging between my face and Takira's.

"A little," Takira mumbles.

A little is accurate, since we only had one night before everything went to shit, but that doesn't feel like the *whole* truth. Doesn't tell the story of how we talked about real things on the roof that night, sketching our dreams in the sky with stars. As irrational as it is, when our glances lock, I see that awareness, the memory of that one night, in Takira's eyes. She pulls back, but my hands tighten reflexively at her hips. It's instinct to hold on to her. Not one I want to examine too closely, but she angles a sharp look up at me, her curves still pressed into the length of my body. Reluctantly, I let her go.

Even though she's taller than average, her head doesn't quite clear my shoulder. It makes me want to protect her even if it's only from falling. Seeing her for the first time in more than a decade, it's a ridiculous response, but that same connection I felt with her from the beginning is undeniable. Given a little time and attention, I bet it could grow into whatever it could have been had things not happened the way they did. That night before the championship, Cliff told our team that game would change everything. He probably was thinking of himself…because he always did, but it changed everything for *me*. As much as I've always been grateful for the chance that led me to a career in the League, I've also felt guilt over how things went down for Cliff. Any possibility for something with his sister fell apart that night along with everything else.

"I want to hear all about how you know each other later. Right now, he's your first model," Lotus says, nodding to the seat and mirror right behind me. "Naz, sit. I think just a little powder and a haircut for him."

"I just got a haircut," I protest.

"I mean a good one." Lotus grins, mischief in her dark eyes.

I grumble but sit obediently in the chair because Lotus may be tiny, but she's a bulldozer. Takira closes her eyes briefly and blows out a breath before pasting on a polite smile.

"Cat," Lotus says, her smile fading. "Let's go check those dresses that just arrived. I hope we got the sizes right. No time for mistakes today."

"Right." Catalina's eyes widen, and she trails Lotus's marching figure, casting a look over her shoulder. "I'll see you later, Takira. You did say you can make the after-party, right?"

Takira's mouth forms an O, and her glance slides to me before lowering to the floor. "Um, yeah, but now I'm not sure I—"

"You're coming!" Lotus yells from a foot or so ahead, turning backward and narrowing her eyes at Takira. "I want all the *Dessi Blue* gossip, and I have some other stuff coming up I'd love to discuss."

She turns to walk off, but not before giving me a discreet wink. Am I that obvious? Or is Lotus that omniscient? According to Kenan, nothing gets by his wife, and she knows things about you before you know them yourself.

Thank you, Lo.

The prospect of getting to talk to Takira at the party tonight lightens a mood that has been admittedly foul all day. I hate stuff like this. MacKenzie Decker, San Diego Waves' president of basketball operations, says he's only met one player less enthused about doing press and the public than me, and that's Kenan Ross. People often draw comparisons between Kenan and me. When he retired, I was traded to the Waves and have never been happier with a team. Kenan has been a big part of that. He mentors lots of young players, and though after eight seasons, I'm not considered young, Kenan's still about ten years older than me. There's a lot I can learn from him, and he and Lotus have become close friends.

Which brings me back to the good turn Lotus inadvertently did me by recruiting Takira Fletcher for this fashion show. For Takira to also be doing my makeup…wait a minute.

"I don't need makeup," I tell Takira, who's setting up little pots of blush and trays of eye shadow. Is that lipstick?

Oh, hell, no.

"It won't be much," she promises, her small smile tentative. "Powder to get rid of the shine. A little eyebrow grooming."

She considers my head, narrowing one eye. "And Lo's right. I'll edge you up."

"I always cut my own hair."

"I can tell." Her husky chuckle disarms me, rolls over my skin leaving a trail of goose bumps the same way it did when we were eighteen years old. "You actually do a good job. I've never seen you less than well-groomed. We just want it freshly cut for the show."

"When did you see me do a good job? With my hair, I mean."

The question lands between us with a thud. She's facing the mirror, arranging her tools, and her hands pause for a second. I watch her reflection, the way her expression freezes before sliding into a grimace.

"Oh, um…I saw you on television," she says, her hands busy again. "Like a press conference on TV after a game, in a few magazines, sports highlights. Stuff like that."

I'm not sure which view I enjoy more. When she's turned away from me, and I can appreciate the long lines of her legs encased in tight black denim, and the two overripe globes of her ass, or the front view. When she faces me again, my eyes involuntarily drop to her breasts, bigger, rounder than they were senior year. To be expected. She's put on weight in perfect places. Hips, thighs, butt, breasts. I thought she was fantastic before. If possible, she's bigger and better. Slim and thick. Lush and tight with braids falling to graze the small of her back. Holding her for just a few seconds proved she's as soft as she looks. She's not little. Not a woman you'd have to hold back with. Not a girl you'd be afraid to break if you fucked her hard.

It's very quiet with only my lascivious thoughts speaking to me as Takira leans against the small counter, arms folded under her breasts, brows raised.

"Should I turn in a slow circle?" she asks mildly. "In case there is one part of my body you didn't get to ogle? Maybe you missed a spot. I'm sure you could accurately guess my cup size by now."

"I wasn't—"

"Oh, you weren't checking me out?"

"No, I *was*," I admit unabashedly. "I was gonna say I actually wasn't done, so a slow circle would be great."

"Oh, my god. You—"

"And I wouldn't miss a spot."

That shuts her up. Her pretty, pouty lips purse. Her eyes narrow before she rolls them and turns back to the mirror and the items spread out on the counter. She walks behind me to drape a protective plastic cape over my shoulders. We both fall silent while she edges me up with her clippers, the occasional brush of her fingers at my neck and ears sending a jolt to my dick. Fortunately, years of discipline playing at an elite level keep me from making a complete fool of myself. I rest my hands casually in my lap so the slight rise of my erection won't be too noticeable.

"So you did it, huh?" I ask when she's finished with my hair and putting the clippers away.

She plucks a case of powder from the array of makeup on the counter, meeting my eyes briefly in the mirror.

"I did what?" She turns back to me with a wipe in her hand.

"You told me that night before the game you wanted to do hair. Looks like all your dreams came true."

The wipe she's gently passing over my face stills at the words "before the game," and I kick myself for even bringing it up. She resumes wiping my skin clean and tosses the used wipe to the nearby trash can.

"I still have a few dreams left." She lifts my chin and dusts my face with powder.

"Is this really necessary?"

"It's for shine," she says, smiling but not looking at me, which is good because my gaze is fixed on her breasts at eye level while she's applying the powder.

It's feeling like puberty all over again. I'm not one of those ballers who has a different girl every night. I get my share, but it's never out of control. When I'm fucking someone, I feel good, of course, but it's all below the belt. Seeing Takira again stirs other parts of me, just like she did the one night we had together on that roof. All the things I'd like to do to her, with her, run through my mind now like they did then. Only then they seemed...possible. After what happened at the championship game, I thought none of those things could ever happen. Hell, Cliff basically told me they couldn't. Now, though, all these years later, we're older, and maybe old wounds have healed enough that new possibilities could rise.

"Which dreams do you have left?" I ask, drawing my brows together when she spreads something cool and gelatinous over them.

"Stop frowning." She laughs. "I'm trying to set your brows."

"Completely necessary to walk out there for two minutes wearing whatever Lotus puts on me," I say wryly. "Which dreams?"

"Oh, I don't know." She sighs, pauses, and fixes her eyes over my shoulder, a wistful look settling onto her pretty face. "My own makeup line. A few other things."

She glances back to me. "What about you? Seems like all your hoops dreams came true."

"Shiiiiit. This has been better than anything I thought I'd ever have. Your brother was the star. I was the backup."

A small awkward silence descends at the mention of her brother, but we can't avoid the subject forever.

"You're doing pretty good for a backup," she says, her tone one of forced lightness.

"And how's Cliff doing?" I ask, watching her face closely. "How's he been?"

"He's better." She lowers her arms, the little wand she was using on my brows dangling from her fingers. "He's actually doing really well. He just got a job coaching at my old high school."

"That's fantastic." The granule of guilt I always feel when I think about Cliff scratches inside me for a second. "I'm really glad to hear that."

"He's, um…" She turns back to the mirror, stowing the tools she used. "He's been clean for a while now. I assume you know about his struggles."

In the mirror, I watch her plump lips pull into a flat line.

"After Sportsco did that disgusting exposé on him and other 'flops,'" she says, bitterness woven into her words, "it triggered a relapse, but he's better now."

Her eyes find mine in the mirror.

"The reporter said you'd been contacted and asked to comment on all the trouble Cliff's had since the championship game." Her expression softens. "Thank you for not giving them anything more than they already had."

They had a lot. The two-hour special documented in painstaking detail why Cliff and several other high school and college basketball phenoms ultimately failed to realize their potential. It was damning, and I wanted nothing to do with it.

"I would never talk about him to the press, or anyone, for that matter," I say, my voice quiet, subdued. "I never have."

"I know."

Our eyes hold, and the space separating us heats, shrinks until even though she's more than a foot away, it feels like there's only a breath between us. Her chest rises and falls on a deep inhale. She licks her lips, almost nervously, and I can't help myself. My eyes greedily track the movement, how she wets her bottom lip with her little pink tongue. Before my brain can wander to all the places I'd like that tongue to be, someone breaks the spell we're under. Or at least, I am under.

"Are you Takira?" a tall girl with pink hair asks, stepping into our space. "Catalina sent me over for makeup."

"Um, yeah." Takira nods briskly. "I was just finishing up with someone."

Pink Hair's eyes wander to me, over me, and her grin goes wicked. "Well, hello, Mr. Armstrong. Ballers, ballers, everywhere. I'll be at the after-party later if you're looking for company."

"I'll be there." I stand, removing the little smock tied around my neck to cover my clothes, and look down into Takira's guarded eyes. "But I hope I'll be busy catching up with an old friend."

Takira doesn't respond, but that's okay. I don't need her to. She gets started on Pink Hair's makeup. If Takira doesn't show up for the after-party, I'll find her. After all these years and all that's happened, we owe ourselves that.

Chapter Four

Takira

What are the odds?

Whatever they are, they're against me. Of all people to sit down in my chair at today's fashion show, an event I wasn't even originally booked for...Nazareth Armstrong.

I'd be lying if I said I hadn't thought of him often over the years. How could I not? Every milestone of his career he celebrated, my brother bemoaned. Sometimes the amazing turns his life took were the very things that sent Cliff on his worst benders. When Naz's team won the championship a few years ago, giving him a ring before the age of thirty, Mama couldn't find Cliff for days. I flew home to help search because she was so desperate. The boy who was once her greatest source of pride has delivered the most sorrow to her door.

"Thank you again for stepping in today," Catalina says, sipping her drink, the lights from the pool in Lotus's backyard casting a glow on her face.

"Oh, thanks for asking." I swirl the pomegranate martini in my glass. "It was fun."

It had been. Not having done a fashion show in a while, I'd forgotten the rush of adrenaline that comes with the lightning-fast outfit changes and look adjustments. I practically launched a few models down the runway when time was tight.

"Takira!" Lotus calls from a few feet away. She's changed and now wears a dress so short it exposes what looks like lace stockings tattooed around the tops of her thighs. The tiny straps show off the delicate line of her collarbone, and her platinum braids contrast perfectly against the rich brown of her face. Her round belly should appear incongruous in the sexy outfit with the strappy heels, but she manages to look effortlessly glamorous and comfortable in her own skin.

"I'm so glad you came," she says, drawing even with Catalina and me. "Thanks for helping out today and for coming tonight."

"Hey, Hollywood party filled with beautiful people. It didn't take much convincing," I joke.

Actually I *did* have to convince myself to come. Seeing Naz changed everything. There's still something magnetic between us, striking sudden and sure the same way it did the night he walked into my mama's house on the eve of the big game. Loyalty to my brother, concern for his fragile recovery urged me to make my excuses, hightail it back to my studio apartment, and forget the random encounter with the man Cliff hates more than anyone else.

Yet here I am, planted by the pool and scanning the crowd for a glimpse of the towering man with intense eyes and a fresh haircut.

"I wanted you to meet my cousin Iris," Lotus says, tugging forward a woman I've seen many times with her famous baller husband, August West.

"Thank you for helping out today," Iris says, her voice low and even. There's a tough kind of serenity to her. Lotus's strength and power are so much a part of her it seems she was born into them. Iris, with her very public battle as a survivor, won her strength by walking through hell and coming out the other side whole.

"I loved every minute of it," I reply to Iris. "I hope Harbor House got everything they needed."

Excitement brightens Iris's eyes, and she smiles so wide, it's easy to see why her husband is notoriously devoted to her. Conviction makes her glow even more.

"We passed our goal, yes," she says. "Thanks for asking. You live here in LA?"

"I do now," I say. "Relocated from New York a while back to work on a movie and ended up staying on the West Coast."

"The *Dessi Blue* movie," Lotus pipes up.

"I can't wait for that one," Iris says, curiosity reshaping her expression. "So were you born in New York?"

"Oh, no. I was born in Trinidad, but my parents moved us to Houston when I was still a baby."

"You ever go back?" Catalina asks.

"All dee time, gyal," I say, slipping on my mother's accent like a pair of familiar slippers. "My sister Janice and I go to Carnival every chance we get."

"I've been a few times," Lotus says. "I actually want to name my summer line Carnival, inspired by the vibrant colors and the flamboyant costumes. I've already sketched out a few things and talked to my team about maybe shooting the campaign in Trinidad."

"Are you kidding?" I gasp. "That would be amazing. Maybe you could even connect with the tourist board. They'd love that kind of exposure with a brand as popular as yours."

"You think?" Lotus asks, eyes wide.

"I'm sure."

"It'll have to wait until this little guy pops out," Lotus says, touching her belly with obvious tenderness.

"It's a boy?" I ask.

"Yes." She rolls her eyes. "Can't tell Kenan nothing. He has a girl, my stepdaughter, Simone, from his first marriage. He would have been happy no matter what, but getting a boy? Yeah, he's over the moon."

"August was the same way," Iris says, kicking off her shoes and sitting on the edge of the pool.

"How many kids do you have?" I ask her.

"Two." She lowers her feet into the water. "But some days it feels like twelve. August is amazing when he's home, but he's gone so much during the season. We have onsite daycare at my job for David. He starts kindergarten next year and Sarai's already in elementary school, but it's still a lot solo."

"Can't say I miss Kenan being on the road half the year," Lotus says.

"I thought August would sink into a depression when Kenan left," Iris says. "Thank God they brought Naz in."

"That reminds me." Lotus turns inquisitive eyes my way. "How did you say you and Nazareth know each other, Takira?"

The sudden silence encompasses our lounging circle, swelling with the three women's collective curiosity.

"Oh, yeah, well." I stall, staring into my now-empty glass. "He and my brother played ball together in high school. We haven't seen each other in years."

"He seemed mighty glad to 'see' you." Catalina snickers.

I shoot her a sharp look but don't say anything.

"And he's never glad to see anyone," Lotus adds, eyeing me. "I feel like there's a story there. Come on. You can tell us."

"There really isn't," I rush to correct them. "I literally met Naz once. He only transferred to my brother's prep school senior year, so they didn't have much time together before graduation. I'm surprised he even remembered me."

Now that's a lie. Even though we only met once, I have no doubt I left an impression on him, as he left one on me. Kindness and intelligence and curiosity. Hell, he was the first man to ever make me come. The way he made me feel, it lingered long after he had left Houston to follow his dreams.

"He's here somewhere," Iris says, craning her neck to look out over the crowd.

"Last I saw him," Lotus says, "he was playing pool with Kenan and August. They'll be over soon, I'm sure. Kenan can only be separated from this baby for like an hour at a time."

We laugh, but an urgency to leave assails me. I can't deny the attraction when I saw Naz today, but somehow I know, if I actually do see him again, I'll get drawn into an impossible situation. One that could become a tug of war between my loyalty to Cliff and the attraction that's still there between Naz and me.

"Where's your restroom?" I ask, standing abruptly. "I gotta go."

"Oh, sure." Lotus gestures toward the house with one whole side comprised of wide windows open and overlooking the pool and backyard. "Down that hall off the foyer, first door on the right."

"Thanks." I split a smile between the three of them. "I'll be right back."

I probably won't be. I do have to use the restroom, but I'll find a way to slip out after that and call Catalina tomorrow using a headache as an excuse for my disappearance. Lotus mentioned possibly working together. We exchanged numbers, and hopefully something will come of it, but I need to get out of here. I pick my way around the pool with careful steps, feeling slightly lightheaded after a few drinks from the bar. I do my business and wash my hands, fully prepared to tiptoe my ass right outta here. Naz makes me do something none of the Groundhog dates ever have.

Feel.

I feel…confused, unsure. Exhilarated. Turned on.

All I've wanted the last few years was to feel, and now that I do, it's with the wrong guy. A guy who has, through no fault of his own, hurt my brother so badly. Cliff is finally clean. Finally getting better. I can't risk a connection with the very man he blames for his misfortune, even if that blame is completely misplaced.

I dry my hands and head back into the hall, determined to get out of here, only to run, for the second time today, into a wall of muscle and man.

I glance up and up until my eyes collide with Naz's. He stares down at me, his hands coming to my elbows, gripping there to steady me. That mere touch sends my heartbeat into an erratic pattern and quickens my breath. He runs his thumbs along the backs of my arms in a gentle caress.

"There you are," he says, his eyes intent, his mouth unsmiling as if he knows exactly what I was about to do. That I was leaving to escape this very moment and this very man. "I've been looking for you."

Chapter Five

Naz

Damn.

I didn't get to see Takira blossom from the girl I met in high school into the gorgeous, confident woman standing in front of me. Thanks to social media and my nagging curiosity, I got to see some things from a distance. I kept loose tabs on Cliff. None of what happened was my fault, but he clearly laid blame at my feet. I sometimes looked for ways I might help, might be able to intervene with some opportunity that would get him back on track, but he snorted and shot up all his chances. You can't save an addict from himself. Ultimately, he has to do that, but every time Cliff occurred to me, so did his sister.

"Naz," Takira says, blinking up at me in surprise. "Hey."

"I was looking for you earlier. Thought you might be hiding from me."

"Hiding?" She twists her lips into a grimace. "Not unless chilling by the pool is considered hiding."

"So you weren't about to leave without saying goodbye?"

She glances down, her smile chagrined. "Well, maybe I was about to do that."

Mascaraed lashes paint shadows on her cheeks. Her makeup is flawless—vibrant blue and green and purple eye shadow, fuchsia-colored lips, dark, dramatic brows winging over her bright eyes. A strapless body suit lovingly molds every breakneck curve and bold line. Her shoulders, a rich shade of mahogany, gleam under the warm overhead light in the hall. Her arms look strong, but soft and rounded. A small diamond "T" dangles from a gold chain linked around the slim column of her neck and rests in the shallow well at the base of her throat.

My assessment of her is leisurely and thorough. I'm taking my time and taking in every detail down to her backless high heels and the nude color painted on her toes. I've never been a foot man, but she could convert me to any part of her body with just a crook of her finger. She's obviously a woman who invests in herself, who takes care of herself. As a man who makes a living taking care of my body, I appreciate this. Any man who wins a woman like Takira would be blessed.

"Damn, Naz," Takira huffs out a laugh. "You always this bold with it? You don't be trying to hide your interest, do you?"

"I'm rarely this interested."

Her dark eyes snap up to mine, searching for the truth I know is there.

"I gotta go," she says, not addressing my last comment.

"Could I get your number? You live in LA now, right? Maybe we could—"

"I don't think so." She slides her eyes to a point over my shoulder. "That's probably not a good idea."

"Why not?"

"I think you know."

We stare at each other, stewing in the shared memory, not only of the night we bared our hopes to each other but of the night that followed. The night that changed everything for me and for Cliff.

A couple stumbles down the hall, kissing and not really paying attention. They bump into me and pull apart to study us.

"Sorry." The woman giggles, her blue eyes a little glassy. I recognize her as one of the models from today's show.

"You finished in there?" The guy nods to the bathroom where Takira stands in the door.

"Oh." Takira steps out of the way, clearing their path. "Yeah, sorry."

"Thanks," the model says, grabbing her partner's hand and dragging him inside, slamming and locking the door behind them.

"I think that's my cue to go," Takira says, turning to head up the hall.

I grasp her wrist, being careful with the strong, slim bones captured between my fingers. She looks from that point of contact between us up to my face.

"Five minutes," I say.

She blows out a long sigh, her expression resigned, and nods. "Five."

A few people wander into the hall to wait for the bathroom. Judging by the grunts and pants coming through that door, they might be waiting a minute. I don't miss the speculative glances some send my way. You don't catch me chasing *nobody*. A monk I'm not, but you won't find me trending. I keep a low profile. So me standing in the hall practically *petitioning* a woman for five minutes of her time… I don't need folks in my business like that.

Not releasing Takira's wrist, I lead her farther down the hall and to a flight of stairs. I glance over my shoulder to meet the question in her eyes.

"Just a little privacy," I tell her. "There's a place downstairs."

After a small pause, she nods and allows me to continue. The stairwell empties into the billiard room. I was down here with Kenan and some of the guys earlier playing pool, but they all went to find their girls. Lucky for me, the room is now empty. I lean against the pool table, and she works her wrist free from my loosened grip. Putting some space between us, she hops up onto the edge of the table beside me and kicks her shoes off.

"Sorry," she says, smiling ruefully and wiggling her toes. "Had to. Been on my feet all day."

"You have pretty feet."

I bite my tongue because judging by the half-amused look she angles at me, that was not a normal thing I should have said in this moment. Somehow I've reverted to the awkward kid I was at eighteen.

"Thank you." She yields a grin and leans back on the heels of her palms. "Your five minutes start now."

If I only get five minutes, I'm diving in.

"I called you," I tell her. "After the game, I mean."

"You did?" she asks with a frown.

"Yeah. I didn't have your cell, so I called your house." I huff out a self-deprecating laugh. "I guess I thought even after what happened at the game with Cliff, there might still be a chance for us to hang out. Get to know each other."

"I didn't know you called," she says softly.

"Yeah. The first time, Cliff answered." I chuckle without any real humor. "You can imagine how that went."

"His anger with you was unjustified." She looks at me squarely. "You didn't punch that coach. Cliff did, and it cost him everything. Well, it cost him a chance at division-one ball. The bad decisions he made after that—the drugs—they cost him everything else."

"I knew he had a temper. We all knew, but I never expected him to lose it like that."

With thirty seconds left in the first half of the biggest game of his life, Cliff Fletcher punched our opponent's coach so hard he fell to his knees. He was black-balled on every list after that. No coach, no college would touch him.

"It *was* a bad call by the ref," Takira admits dryly. "But no foul, no call is worth your future. Cliff didn't have to go HAM on that ref, and he didn't have to punch that coach in the face."

She bites her lip, flicking a glance to me beside her, propped against the pool table.

"You were ready for the moment, Naz," she says. "I don't even think Coach Lipton knew you could play the way you did when he subbed you after halftime."

"Real talk, *I* didn't know I could play like that."

I shove my hands in my pockets, uncomfortable with the contrast between how my career soared after that high school championship and how everything soured for her brother. "If you remember, I had actually been talking to the coach from my old high school to see if I might get some looks for football. I didn't think I'd proven myself enough in basketball to get any real college consideration."

"When Cliff got thrown out and you had to step up, you did. Big time."

I had a triple double and played more aggressively than I ever had. Cliff was such a hot prospect the game was being televised. So everyone and their grandma saw Cliff punch that coach. The scouts who had come out to see Cliff saw me instead, playing the game of my life. The offers that should have gone to him came to me. They saw me step in for him and play like my life depended on it. Considering how Mama's hospital bills had piled up, maybe my life—and hers—*had* depended on it.

"I was happy for you," Takira says, reaching over to take my hand and give it a squeeze. "I knew what that opportunity meant for you and your family. I knew you'd make the most of it."

And I did.

When a few offers for division-one colleges rolled in, I chose a full ride at the school with the best business program.

"You know," I say, stroking my thumb over the smooth skin of her hand, "even once I got to State, I didn't ever expect to start. I thought I'd ride the bench for four years and get my degree paid for. That's all I really wanted at first."

"But you got there and did what you always seem to do. You learned, you got better, you never gave up, and it landed you not only in the League, but with a championship. While Cliff..." She looks away and bites her lip. "Well, he gave up really badly. You didn't punch that coach. You didn't force my brother to turn to drugs when all he had worked for dried up. You didn't ruin his life, but he needed someone other than himself to blame."

"So he blamed me," I finish for her. "When I called the week after the game, he was furious and told me to stay away from you."

"He told me the same thing." She shrugs. "You and I only had one conversation, so when you didn't call—"

"Except I did. Twice. The second time your mother said she thought it best I not call again. Not for Cliff." I hold her stare. "And not for you."

"Can't say I'm surprised. The punch was on every sports channel. Reporters were in our front yard. Colleges that had made offers withdrew them immediately." She shakes her head and sighs. "If they weren't talking about how bad Cliff had screwed up, they were talking about how you *stepped* up."

"I'm sorry."

I'm not sorry for anything I *did*, but for how things went so badly for him.

"Talking with you, going out with you—*anything* with you right after it happened," she says, "would have felt like a betrayal to Cliff."

"I get it. You had to focus on your family." I shrug. "To be honest, so did I. My mom was only getting worse, and the bills weren't going anywhere. I had to make the most of that opportunity for her and my sisters."

"Which is exactly where your focus should have been. I mean, yeah, you and I had a great conversation on that roof and—"

"We did more than talk," I remind her with a wry smile.

She had said I was the first to make her come. That should count for *something*.

Her eyes snap to mine, a slow smile kissing her lips. "True, and it was…great. It really was, but he's my brother, and he was at his lowest point. Going out with you would have been salt in the wound."

"I get that," I say, nodding. "I wish things could have been different, but I get it."

"You're a trigger for him. When you got drafted into the League, he was so bitter. He went on one of his worst trips that week. And when you won your ring…" She shakes her head and closes her eyes. "It was bad. When they did that stupid documentary, he was so upset, we almost lost him."

"What do you mean?" I ask with a quick frown.

"He overdosed," she says, her voice hushed, her eyes haunted. "He flatlined, and they revived him. It almost killed Mama, too."

Hearing that, I'm horrified. I know it's not my fault, but guilt saws my insides nonetheless. I push away from the table and move to face her, standing in front of her still seated on the table's edge. "I had no idea."

"He's lost everything, Naz. He has two kids with a good woman, but she left when he spiraled again. She had just been through too much. She's with another guy now, and Cliff is finally getting access to the kids again. He's piecing things back together."

"I reached out a few times in the past, but he was never receptive." I take both her hands in mine. "But if there's anything I can ever do to help, let me know."

"Maybe give up on this idea of us going out," she says softly, half-hopefully.

"We shouldn't have to." I tighten my grip on her fingers and shake my head, holding her eyes with mine. "I get why then it was bad timing, but maybe now...it could be right."

She sucks her teeth but makes no move to pull her hands away. "It's not worth the drama it'll cause if Cliff finds out."

"Not worth it to who?" I ask, stepping closer, filling the small space between her knees. With one finger, I lift her chin, caressing the tiny indentation bisecting the delicate surface. "I'd like to at least see if it could be worth it to me."

Even now, this close, the pull between us is strong, vital. I lean forward, never dropping her eyes from mine, giving her plenty of time to pull away, to push me away, if she chooses.

She doesn't choose.

The shorter the distance between our lips, the closer I get, the shorter her breaths come, shallow pants that lift her breasts and coast past her full lips. I'm so close now, we exchange a ragged sigh, my mouth hovering over hers.

"I'mma kiss you now," I whisper. "Unless you tell me not to."

Her silence stretches between us, and her lashes drop to cover the emotions swimming in her eyes—curiosity, lust, need.

Guilt.

I press a soft kiss to the corner of her mouth, nibble at the full curve of her bottom lip, lick the delicately drawn bow at the top. She gasps, her mouth opening the smallest bit. I take immediate advantage, licking into her, seeking and finding the sweet, slick interior. She moans, and I suck on her tongue, at first gentle, and then incited by the whimpers slipping from her throat, harder.

I cup her face between my hands, thumbing the smooth skin of her cheeks. The cadence of the kiss changes, intensifies as our movements become more hurried, more desperate. I slide my palms down her neck, over her shoulders and back.

"You feel good," I mutter against her lips.

I kiss across her cheek and behind her ear, drawing in the clean scent tucked into the cove for me there. "You smell good."

I trail kisses down her throat, taking the satiny skin between my lips and nipping lightly with my teeth. "You taste good."

She arches her neck back, offering herself to me.

"I'd like to spend some time with you," I whisper in her ear. "The date we never got before."

She stiffens, pulling back and closing her eyes, her lips still swollen from my bites and kisses. "Naz, I can't."

"Takira, don't be ridiculous."

"I'm not being ridiculous." Shaking her head, she hops off the table, pushes past me, and grabs her shoes, hooking the heels over one hand. "I'm choosing my brother."

She walks away swiftly, but it takes no time to catch her. With legs as long as mine, one of my steps equals two of hers. I take her by the elbow at the base of the stairs, turning her to face me.

"That's not the real choice, Takira. Not me or him. It's just you and me. He's a grown man who's experienced incredible disappointment and made a lot of mistakes. I sympathize with that, but he can't expect you to pay for them. That's not fair."

"It doesn't make sense, his anger at you," she says, tugging her elbow free. "His grudge against you isn't fair, but you're a trigger for him, and he almost died. Didn't you hear me?"

"I heard you say he's been clean for a long time and has a new job."

"Exactly, and I don't want jeopardize that because you're an itch I never got to scratch."

"Oh, we're gonna scratch, Kira."

My words come out soft and certain in a way she may not recognize, but I do. It's the tone I've heard from myself when I want something badly, I'll do whatever it takes to get it. I willed myself to reach beyond my skill the night I subbed for Cliff. I pushed myself all through college so I would shine hidden among brighter, better talents. It's what I required of myself to go from a second-round draft pick to an all-star who, against all odds, won a ring in the League when most never do.

At my words, low and determined, she pauses, one bare foot on the step, and considers me over her shoulder. She doesn't want me? Fine. But she didn't kiss me like a woman who didn't want me back.

Whatever she sees in my eyes, it makes worry knit her fine brows together, and she runs, taking the steps quickly to the next floor before I can warn her that I *will* chase.

I let her go for now. Over the years, I've learned when to pursue and when to fall back, biding my time and playing the long game. Twelve years is a very long game. It was one kiss. One conversation. *That* I could walk away from. I did. But the kiss we just had? The attraction simmering between us...*that* is worth exploring. This isn't about then. It's about *now.*

I follow more slowly, and as expected, there's no sign of Takira when I reach the foyer. I glance through the front door someone is holding open and see her standing outside. I watch her for a few moments before an Uber pulls up and she leaves. I'll figure out my next step later. There's a pattern in my life. Yes, I'm always ready, prepared when the moment comes, but opportunities have a habit of presenting themselves to me. I'm just the guy who recognizes when they come and knows how to make the most of them. Pundits have often drawn parallels between my career and guys like Tom Brady, who, as a sixth-round draft pick, was the back-up quarterback. When the starter Drew Bledsoe was injured, Brady had to step in. Seven Superbowl rings later, the rest, as they say, is history. Preparation meeting opportunity. Discipline making up for deficits. That's always been my calling card, too.

I wander outside, grinning when I see my friends lounging by the pool. Lotus is perched on Kenan's knee. Iris and August are stretched out, entwined on a lounge chair, holding hands.

"You guys are sickeningly sweet," I say in mock disgust, flopping into an empty chair at the table beside Kenan and Lotus.

"How will you survive all this disgusting sweetness on our bae-cation?" Lotus asks, biting Kenan's ear and waggling her brows at me.

"Oh, you mean the geriatric cruise." I chuckle. "Also known as Kenan's fortieth birthday party?"

"You don't want a free two-week ride on a yacht in the Mediterranean?" Kenan grumbles, tucking his chin into the curve of Lotus's neck. "Stay your ass at home."

"Yeah, Naz," August says, standing and walking over from the lounge chair. "It'll be all couples, and we know how awkward that could be for you since you haven't had a meaningful relationship in, oh...ever."

"He has a very meaningful relationship," Kenan deadpans, "with his trainer."

"Stop teasing him," Iris chides, joining us at the table. "It's not his fault he has commitment issues."

"I do not have commitment issues." I laugh, leaning the chair back on two legs.

"He just hasn't found the right person," Lotus says, narrowing her eyes in that way she has that makes you feel like she's peeled your skin back and found something interesting. "Though he was all up in Takira's personal space today."

"You don't know what you're talking about." I look over the infinity pool, not meeting the curious eyes of my friends. "Tell me more about this cruise we're going on. Who's coming?"

"Well, the four of us, obviously. And there's…" Lotus counts on her fingers silently. "Six couples."

"And you." August grins.

"You could always bring a plus one," Lotus says.

"I don't have a…" The rest of my denial gets lost in a jumble of thoughts as a brilliant plan emerges. One that formulates as yet another opportunity presents itself.

"So, Lotus," I say, tossing her a devious grin. "Does she have to *know* she's my plus one?"

Chapter Six
Takira

I drank too much and didn't fuck enough.

Correction. I didn't fuck *at all*, and it's been so long that I'm feeling it. My head pounds, and my pussy throbs. She's mad at me for walking away from what could have been—*but now we'll never know*—the best dick of my life. Maybe Naz wouldn't deliver on that kiss, but the way he took my tongue in his mouth and sucked hard while his big hands were so gentle at my throat, on my shoulders, arms, back? That was a man who knew what he was doing, and he wanted to do it to me.

And I'll be damned if I didn't want to let him.

"Shit."

I roll onto my back and slide a hand into my panties beneath the coolness of the sheets. As soon as I got home, I downed quite a bit of wine, hoping to take off the edge Naz pushed me to. I peeled that bodysuit off, tossed my Jimmy Choos into a corner, and crawled in bed bare. I woke up soaked from dreams of that man, a collage of the past, the present, and the future he gave me a glimpse of last night with a mere kiss. A future where he fucks me like I've been wanting, needing for a long time. I like it hard and deep and nasty.

No apologies. No shame.

My sister even got me a vibrator for Christmas. My people *know*. None of those Groundhog dates have led to anything—not only no relationships, but no hook-ups. I love sex, but I'm discriminating. Not just anyone is getting up in here, and so far, I haven't been impressed by the LA buffet.

The last great orgasm I wasn't personally responsible for occurred two weeks ago at an industry party. There was this girl…Janna, I think. Her name is fuzzy. The way that chick robo-tongued me for like an hour—that part is crystal clear. She left no crumbs. I find women tend to take their time—to be attuned to your body's responses. Once they find a spot, they *stay* there. It would be really convenient if I didn't also like to be filled, like, to the brim with dick. If I didn't like a man's rough hairs abrading my legs and crave that weight on top of me, behind me. If I didn't like to wake up tucked into the solid bulk of a man at my back, but I do. I've given and received to all and enjoyed it all. I want to feel good with people I like and respect. Whatever you call that, that's what I am. Bisexual. *Sexual.* Others can choose to label it. I just live it.

I work my clit, slick and swollen between my legs, trail the other hand up my torso to squeeze my breast, pluck at one nipple. My body responds, but there's something detached about this. Something almost mechanical that leaves me cold inside even as parts of me go hot. I give up, jerking my hand from my panties and letting it fall by my head in a clenched fist.

Naz's handsome face keeps crowding my thoughts. That kiss—hot, commanding, tender—has me shook. Left me wanting something I can't quite put my finger on, no pun intended. It's more than just sex. It's curiosity. It's fascination. Excitement. I can't name all the emotions Naz sparked in me last night, but I know they picked up from where they left off that night so many years ago. We talked and made out that night, sure, but we were just kids. Last night—that was some grown folks shit, and I've rarely—if ever—felt an attraction that intense.

My phone on the bedside table rings, jarring me from the smutty mire of my thoughts. I unplug it from the charger and bring it to my ear, not bothering to check who's calling.

"Hello," I yawn into the phone, swiping a hand down my face and frowning at the black and fuchsia smears on my palm. I broke the cardinal rule of makeup removal last night.

"Me sistah," Janice, my eldest sibling, drawls from the other line, exaggerating her island lilt. She actually does have a little bit left from living in Trinidad longer than I did and learning to talk while she was there. "What are you doing this fine morning?"

"Nothing much." I sit up and prop my back against the headboard. "Just laying around, looking like yesterday."

"How'd the fashion show go? You see any celebrities?"

"A few. I met Lotus Ross, of course."

"I love her stuff."

"Same." I lick my lips before going on. "There were lots of basketball players there. Her husband, Kenan, had recruited a lot of his friends, so I met a few ballers."

I pause, tugging the sheet up to cover my breasts. I've never told Janice about that one night with Naz. I was especially hesitant when it became clear what a sore subject he became for Cliff, and by extension, the rest of my family.

"You know this old married lady lives vicariously through you, Tee. Please tell me you smashed some rich, famous, fine-ass baller."

I get out of bed, slipping a short silk robe on over my thong. Leaving it to hang open, I pad barefoot to the kitchen.

"How about a kiss?" I ask, not sure how much I should tell her or how she'll respond. She knows as well as I do how Cliff feels about Naz.

"Who was it? Anybody I know?"

"Um…" I start my coffee machine. "Nazareth Armstrong?"

For a few extended seconds, the drip of my coffee is the only sound. Is she even breathing?

"Hellooo?" I ask, forcing a laugh. "Is this thing on?"

"You saw Naz? You *kissed* Naz?"

"Wasn't the first time," I mutter, fitting the phone between my ear and shoulder to grab yogurt from the fridge.

"What does that mean? What you 'bout, Tee?"

"The night before the championship game, Cliff had the team over for dinner."

"Yeah, and?"

"That's the night I met Naz, and something clicked with us. We talked for hours up on the roof."

"And you kissed him?"

"Yeah, and it was like… I don't know. Girl, it was like magic." I chuckle self-consciously, knowing how fanciful I must sound to my notoriously pragmatic older sister.

"Why am I just now hearing 'bout this?"

"Really, Neecey? Naz's name was mud in our house. It's not like he and I had a relationship. We had a connection. It felt real and good and like potential, but after what happened, I couldn't do that to Cliff."

"And you just ran into him at the show after all this time?"

"I literally tripped and fell into his arms." I pour a generous serving of coffee in one of my many *Breakfast at Tiffany's* mugs, this one sporting a sketch of Holly Golightly wearing her sleep mask.

"And you got to talk after the show?"

"There was an after-party at Lotus's house, and he kind of dragged me downstairs to the pool room."

"Did you do it on a pool table?" Janice gasps, and I can't discern if she's outraged or delighted. Probably torn.

"No, I told you we just kissed, but it was like one of those kisses you dream about. It was a lot like the first time we kissed, but he's more confident now. More aggressive."

"And you love that hard shit. Let me guess. That vibrator I gave you for Christmas got a workout last night."

"No."

"This morning?"

"Neecey, will you stop?" I laugh. "Though I must admit…best present ever."

"I also gave you a bottle of rosé. Vibrations *and* libations."

"That rosé *was* bomb, and somehow, even though it's not even my favorite vibe, it's become like my lucky charm." I take a slurpy sip of my coffee. "Even when I go on trips and know I won't use it, I still take it with me."

"Now *that* is weird. All us kids need therapy."

"I feel like we're getting way off topic here. I did not use the vibrator." *I used my hand, and it didn't help.* "But Naz was the last thing I thought about when I went to sleep and the first thing I thought about when I woke up. He wants to see me. Like, take me out or whatever."

"And you said?"

"No, of course."

"Why 'of course'? I'm sick and damn tired of you complaining about the people you meet on Unhinged.com. This is the most excitement I've heard from you ever about anyone."

"It's not that simple, and you know that. Cliff's recovery is so fragile. I don't want to do anything that will set him back."

In the quiet that follows, I imagine she's reliving the horror of Cliff's overdose. We both rushed home, me from LA and Janice from Chicago, where her family lives now. Mama was inconsolable. Daddy was pissed but also terrified.

"I've never been so scared in my life," Janice finally whispers.

"Exactly," I say, taking my coffee back to the bedroom. "I can't do anything to risk that happening again."

"Look, I get it, but we both know Naz had nothing to do with Cliff's shit. He brought that on himself. Why should you ignore an attraction as strong as it sounds like this one is because Cliff might not like it?"

"It's more serious than not liking it," I say, deciding I'm not quite ready to be up and climbing back into bed. "He's obsessed with the idea that Naz took everything that was meant for him and ruined his life. I don't want to send him spiraling."

"Look, at his big age, Cliff is gonna have to get over this. That man is thirty-one years old, has a job, and is looking better than I've seen him in years. Trust that he's getting better, Tee, and take something for yourself. Besides, who says he has to know about it? What's the harm in one date?"

"There's been enough harm done, so I don't plan to find out."

Long after we disconnect, I'm mid-Sunday reset—washing my sheets, wiping down the counters, mopping the floors, and preparing my meals for the week—when the phone rings again. A smile curls on my lips when Lotus Ross's name flashes onscreen.

"Lotus, hey." I leave the kitchen and the whir of my dishwasher, stepping out onto the small balcony with a view that makes this studio worth the rent. "How are you?"

"Recovering," she says, her voice carrying that husky timbre I recognize as exhaustion. "I guess being pregnant really can slow you down, or at least it should, according to my over-protective husband."

"He's so sweet with you. It's nice seeing a man that gone for his wife, especially a professional athlete. You always think of them as dogs, but Kenan is obviously completely devoted."

"He *is* awesome," Lotus agrees softly. "Which actually brings me to the reason for my call."

"Oh, yeah?" I settle onto the wrought-iron chair on my balcony and tip my head back to relish the breeze across my face. "How so?"

"It's his fortieth birthday soon."

I didn't realize there was so much of an age gap between the Rosses. I remember being impressed at all Lotus has accomplished by the age of twenty-nine.

"And we're doing a cruise to celebrate," Lotus continues. "Some of his closest friends on a yacht in the Mediterranean for two weeks. We'll stop in Corsica, Sardinia, Capri, Positano, and Ponz. It should be fantastic."

"That's really cool."

Why is she telling me this?

"I'd love for you to join us."

"Oh...so...huh?" I lean forward to prop my elbows on my knees. "I loved meeting you and Kenan yesterday, but I wouldn't think it qualified me as a close friend."

"Well, I was thinking maybe you could help me while we sail. Remember I said my summer line is Carnival-inspired? I'd love for you to look at what I have so far and maybe brainstorm some other inspirations from the Islands I should consider."

It sounds flimsy, and Lotus is not a flimsy woman. I'm not an aura girl, but Lotus has…something about her that makes you take notice. I've never met a woman with as much presence as she has, commanding a room just by walking into it. So offering me something like this with a trumped-up reason is uncharacteristic.

"What's really going on here, Lotus?" I ask, keeping my voice light so I don't offend her, but also acknowledging that I'm not falling for it.

She huffs out a sigh. "I told him you'd see right through it."

"Him?" I query, sitting up straight with a frown. "Him *who?*"

"Naz. He and Kenan became really close after he went to the Waves when Kenan retired. They also share an agent, Banner Morales. August's agent, his stepbrother Jared, co-owns the agency and is Banner's husband. It's one big happy family. They'll all be on the cruise."

Sounds like a floating who's who, and under normal circumstances, I'd be jumping at the chance to tag along, even if only for the possible networking opportunities. But Naz is so dangerous, so tempting. If I go on this trip, I know how it'll end. Me fucking that man by the first port.

"It's all couples and Naz." Lotus laughs. "Poor thing doesn't have a plus one."

"Don't try to make me feel sorry for him," I joke. "It won't work."

"Look, the man never pursues women like this. He likes you enough to make himself look this desperate, which for a man as proud as he is? That's saying something. I don't want to overstep—"

"But you will," I interject mildly.

"A little, yeah. I got major vibes from the two of you even in the few minutes I saw you at the show together yesterday. I know you had something when you were young."

"High school. It was only one night."

"Looked to me like you wanted one more." Lotus pauses. "Am I wrong?"

"Damn, I knew I liked you," I say, shaking my head. "It's complicated."

"I'mma get personal here for a sec. That all right?"

"Sure. Of course."

"Getting with Kenan was complicated. He had a very public situation with his ex, and she was making it even tougher, on top of bringing custody of his daughter into it. I had my own shit I was dealing with. On the surface, you'd look at our situation and say we should have waited until things were simpler, but I'm glad we didn't. It helped us sort through what was most important to us. It helped us see that we were worth it."

I absorb that in silence, and she goes on.

"And I bet you've heard about Iris and August. Iris's past relationship made national headlines. It gets no more complicated than what Iris and August had to negotiate to be together."

"You guys are married. You're couples. Naz and I barely know each other."

"You should've seen my poor husband the first time he saw me." Lotus lets out a low laugh. "You woulda thought lightning struck that man. The crazy thing was, it struck me, too. You can feel more with the right person in an instant than you've felt with folks you've known all your life. It's not how long you've had together. Maybe it's what you *could* have. I'm just asking if you'd like to find out? And bonus! Sail the Mediterranean eating bomb-ass food and hanging with the most amazing group of friends you ever want to meet? Don't let the belly fool you. Mama still knows how to get down."

I laugh and have no doubt I would love hanging out with Lotus and Iris and their friends for two weeks. They seem like my kind of people. With Neevah and Canon traveling to recoup after the movie wrapped, I don't have many friends in town I know or like to hang with.

And who am I kidding? The greatest draw is that man, Naz. Like Janice said, we can keep it simple, and Cliff won't even have to know. I cannot deny I want to see him again. Kiss him again. And more… Lord, more.

"Can I think about it?" I ask.

"Of course, you can," Lotus says, her tone indulgent. "Honey, you take all the time you like, but I need to know by Tuesday."

I can't help but laugh. Yeah, this whole experience might be worth the risk.

Chapter Seven

Naz

"So let me get this straight," August says, leaning against the rail and looking out over the turquoise water of the Mediterranean. "You meet this girl Takira...what? Twice? And somehow persuade Lotus to invite her on Kenan's birthday cruise as your plus one, but you never actually asked Takira to *be* your plus one?"

"That's about right, yeah." I lean on the rail, too, between him and Jared Foster, my agent's husband.

"I like it," August's brother Jared says, crunching ice between his teeth and swirling the drink in his glass.

"You would," August shoots back.

"What's that supposed to mean?" Jared frowns.

"Dude, you're intense," I offer wryly, not sure how I feel about the comparison to Jared who is known around the League as a shark. "Especially about Banner and your daughter."

"I think that's what they call being a family man," Jared defends himself.

"Or sociopath," August counters. "I've heard both."

Two brothers couldn't be more different. Technically, they're stepbrothers, which accounts for their physical differences—August with dark, curly hair and golden-brown skin juxtaposed against Jared's blond hair and blue eyes. It's the differences in temperament that are most striking. August is a fierce competitor on the court. He has to be as the Waves' team captain once Kenan retired, but he's patient and has a well-earned reputation as one of the nicest guys in the League.

Jared Foster? Different story. One of the most cutthroat agents in the business, he's your classic alpha male. But the dude met his match in my agent, Banner. She's one of the best around, but kind with it. Her reputation as the rookie whisperer was in part what led me to sign with her when I entered the League. Jared was definitely on my list. It worked out, though, because now they own an agency together.

"I'm just saying," Jared continues, the light, warm breeze lifting his hair. "When something or someone is worth wanting, like for real, you go after it…after her. I have a lot of regrets."

He closes one eye and squints up at the cerulean sky for a second.

"Actually. Scratch that. I don't have many regrets," he corrects. "That shit's a waste of time, but of the few regrets I do have, going after Banner with every breath in my body is not one of them. And look what you get."

He pulls out his phone and flips through pics of him and Banner with their daughter, Angela, who is the spitting image of her mother. The three of them are in a swimming pool, and Jared has a giggling Angela hoisted up in the air above his head.

"Thank God Banner had mercy on you and married your ass." August laughs. "No one else would put up with your shit."

Jared's smile fades, but the chiseled lines of his face soften as he stares down at the phone. "Yeah, she was pretty much my one shot."

He angles a look up at me, the softness gone and the usual determined set of his mouth locking in place. "Moral of the story," he says. "When you really want something, pursue."

"Hearing the word 'moral' coming from your mouth," August says, "just feels wrong somehow."

"Fuck you," Jared retorts, slipping the phone back into his pocket.

"That's more like it." August whacks the back of Jared's head and, with an eye roll, Jared yields a grin.

Yeah, they're brothers.

"She's flying in with Kenan and Lotus?" August asks, looking out over the startlingly blue water and the boats of varying sizes bobbing along its surface.

"Yeah." I glance at my watch. "Their plane was supposed to land like thirty minutes ago. They should be boarding soon."

"When I turn forty," August says, flipping around to prop his elbows on the rail and survey the huge deck we're standing on, "remind me to do it on a super yacht with all my friends."

"This thing is massive," I agree. The sun suspended in a cloudless sky glints off the abundance of chrome and the polished wood of the upper deck. "The captain told me it's three hundred-feet long, has six decks, a hammam spa, a twenty-foot pool, and a hot tub."

"There's a helideck," Jared chimes in. "And a screening room. This isn't the first yacht I've been on, but it's for damn sure the best."

"It's like a million a week to charter," August adds. "But Kenan says you only turn forty once."

"He's setting the bar high," I say, taking in the musical fountain on the deck below.

"Yeah, he is." Jared glances at his phone. "Hey, I gotta go. Banner needs me. Probably for sex."

"That's my agent," I grimace. "I don't need to know that shit."

"I fuck your agent all the time." His grin is proud. "And this is totally normal. It's baby hormones. Women get really horny sometimes when they're pregnant."

"Banner's pregnant again?" August asks, mouth dropped open.

"Aw, hell." Jared scrunches up his face. "She wanted to wait and tell you guys at Dad's birthday party next month. Can you pretend to be surprised?"

"Yeah, I guess." He brings Jared in for a quick hug. "Congrats, brother. You caught up with me."

"If Banner gets her way," he says, tilting a rueful smile, "and she always does, we'll pass you soon."

"I'm gonna go check on Iris, too," August tells me once Jared has gone. "It's not her first time being away from Sarai and David, and they're with my mom, but she gets antsy."

"Yeah, I'll head to my room, too. Hanging over the side of the boat waiting and watching for them to arrive ain't helping much."

"Also kinda gives off a stalker vibe."

I level a glare at him.

"You're really this into her after seeing her just a couple times?" he asks, smirking. "I mean, I fell for Iris fast, but it's unusual for you."

We walk along the deck toward the bank of stairs leading down to our rooms.

"It's a little more complicated than that. I've kind of been tracking with her off and on through social media for years."

"Jared would approve." August chuckles.

"Not all the time—just checking on her every once in a while. It's hard to explain, but we had this one night together."

"Like a hook-up?"

"Nah, we were kids. Seniors in high school. We had this conversation on the roof of her house the night before the championship. We kissed, and I just knew we were supposed to be something to each other. I wasn't sure what, but I believed that." I shoot him a sheepish look as we take the stairs. "That probably sounds crazy, huh?"

"Not really." August's expression sobers. "I had that kind of conversation with Iris the night before the NCAA championship, and it changed the course of my life. I *knew* it would, even though I didn't know how. So I get it."

I absorb that information, not feeling quite as ridiculous knowing he experienced something similar. We continue down the passageway, the high-gloss wall paneling and plush carpet underfoot breathing luxury.

"You ever heard of Cliff Fletcher?" I ask, flicking him a sideways glance.

"Where do I know that name from?" August's brows pinch into a frown. "Who's he?"

"He was the biggest thing coming out of Texas high school basketball when I graduated."

"Oh, hell. Yeah. Wasn't he in that SportsCo documentary on flops and fails not too long ago?" August asks. "I remember because they highlighted Len Bias, and if his story ain't a cautionary tale, I don't know what is."

Bias, who many pundits speculate would have been the only true rival to Jordan in that era, overdosed on cocaine two days after being drafted number two overall to the Celtics, becoming the highest draft pick to never play an NBA game. I can't help but draw parallels between the fallen superstar and Cliff, considering the troubles with drugs Takira's brother has experienced.

"That was some bullshit," I say tightly. "Apparently that trash documentary sent Cliff into a spiral and…it was bad."

"They said Fletcher's been in and out of rehab. I remember Avery was pissed. Said that piece was bad journalism and tasteless."

Avery, the wife of our president of basketball operations, is also a lead reporter on SportsCo, one of the biggest sports stations in the world.

"His fall was kind of my rise," I say.

"Damn! That's right. Now I remember. The punch."

"Takira's his sister."

August releases a low whistle, eyes wide and bright with interest.

"That punch gave me my shot," I continue, "and he resents me for every good thing that happened for me after. It's obviously misplaced, but it makes Takira hesitant about giving me a chance. He's been pretty vocal about his disapproval."

"She can't live for her brother."

"Nah, but he's coming off a really bad spiral." I lower my voice even though we're the only ones in the dimly-lit passageway. "After that SportsCo doc, he overdosed and almost died."

"Shit."

"Yeah, so she doesn't want to set him off by getting involved with the guy he apparently hates more than anyone, even if it's baseless."

"Hey, there were times I thought being with the girl I wanted was impossible." August tips his heard toward the door again. "But guess where she is now?"

He grins and fist-bumps me.

"You got her here. That's half the battle. See what two weeks trapped on a ship together gets you."

I laugh and try to shake off any apprehension about the coming meeting. August enters the cabin he shares with Iris, and I continue down the hall toward my room. Takira should be here soon, if not already. My stomach knots at the thought of seeing her again, kissing her again. Talking to her. Finally getting to know her beyond one night on a roof and what I could glean from social media posts.

"It's not that serious," I mutter to myself. "I'm not like in love. I just…"

The words dry up on my tongue because, no. I'm not in love with Takira after so little time and contact, but watching her enter the room beside mine—braids twisted into a crown, a dress the color of tangerines drawn onto her voluptuous body—my heart climbs up my chest and lodges in my throat.

I may not be in love with this girl, but I'm in *something*.

And I'm in deep.

Chapter Eight

Takira

I glance up to see who is coming down the hall as I open the door to my cabin.

"Naz!" I practically screech, pressing both hands to my chest like I'm guarding my heart. Maybe I am because that traitorous organ started a riot behind my rib cage as soon as Naz strode into view. I clutch the doorknob, searching for something to anchor me. So much for my plan to play it cool and indifferent, but I thought I wouldn't see him until dinner. He's here before I've even made it inside my cabin, leaving me no time to prepare. To marshal my defenses against this man.

But there is no defense for fine as fuck, not when it comes swaggering up the hall looking like a whole-ass snack.

"Takira," Naz says, his deep voice pouring over me like hot oil, raising my goose bumps and then singeing them. "I didn't know you were here already. I'm glad you came."

He looks down at me from his great height, nearly a foot above. The breadth of his shoulders blocks out everything behind him, and he's literally the only thing I can see. His scent—clean and woodsy and masculine and uniquely *him*—floods my senses, my nostrils flaring as I breathe him in. Everything about this man screams dominance and confidence, but when his dark eyes latch on to mine, I read a line of uncertainty. We haven't spoken since the after-party, though his wishes, his very clear intentions, are what brought me here.

"This is a pretty elaborate scheme to see me again." I gesture to a porthole in the narrow passageway that flaunts a view of the jewel-like sea. "You could have just asked me out."

"Pretty sure I did and you turned me down."

"And you always get what you want?"

"Usually, yes." A rakish grin crooks one side of his sinfully full lips. "And based on that kiss at Lotus's party, seems like you want me back."

Touché, my brother.

"Well, now that you have me here," I say, allowing a hint of challenge to enter my voice, "do you even know what you want to do with me?"

My words, the taunt erases any tinge of doubt in his stare, and he invades my space, crowding me against the half-open door. Does he realize I lured him this close? That he's exactly where *I* want *him*? I've been around athletes, directors, actors, musicians, powerful men a lot. Men who like to chase and catch. Big, intimidating, commanding—Naz is no different, yet he's like no man I've been with before. He's not even like the Naz I *knew* before.

"I know exactly what I want to do with you." He closes in until his scent and heat curl around me. "You should be asking yourself if you can take it."

My mind and my eyes drift inevitably to the *it* in question, the lengthened steel between his legs, an obvious erection within seconds of being in my presence. A dirty reply waits on my tongue, but when I look back up at him, my breath stalls at his expression. Yes, a devouring hunger roils behind his eyes, and his huge hands curl into fists at his sides like he's two seconds from snatching me up, bending me over the nearest rail, and fucking me senseless. That's all expected, but there's something else. Something *tender* that I'm not sure what to do with. It has no place in a two-week fling, which is all this can be.

I stare up at him, blinking in both confusion and understanding. I'm a romantic at heart. I wouldn't keep trying every dating app known to man if I didn't believe in love—didn't believe there was someone out there for everyone. But even I, horny, heart-y romantic that I am, never imagined a man orchestrating a situation like this just to see me again. And the longer we stand here staring at each other, saying so much without words, the higher the stakes of this thing seem to climb.

"I want to be very clear," I tell him, holding the heated stare that hasn't left my face. "I'm only here for…"

I should say I'm here for the food, the good times, the free trip through the Mediterranean, and to make new famous friends. Hell, I could even say I'm only here for the dick. I could say all of that, but it's not *true.*

At least, it's not the whole truth. I don't completely understand the magnetic pull that sprang up between us when we met all those years ago—don't fully grasp how it endured. I do know it's stronger than anything I've felt with anyone else. It's sharp and deep and quick, like a knife tossed to the bottom of a barrel. It's real, and in a sea of catfish profiles, dead-end dates, and unsolicited dick pics...something real feels like a miracle.

"You were saying you're here for...?" He takes another step forward, urging me farther back. I don't speak but bite my lip and glance down at the floor between us. I've always got something to say, am ready with a comeback, but there are no words for the way he's invaded my thoughts since the fashion show. All the dreams, fantasies this man has spurred are secrets, and I can't bring myself to say any of them out loud.

"How about if I tell you why I brought you here?" he asks, taking another step that backs me over the threshold and into my cabin.

"That's a good idea," I whisper, never breaking our stare. "Tell me."

"Because," he says, kicking the door closed. His wide, warm palm cups my face, and his long fingers brush the nape of my neck. "I can't stop thinking about you."

"You mean since the fashion show?"

He bends until our foreheads touch, his insanely long lashes flicking up to show me the full measure of heat in his eyes. "Longer."

He tips my chin back with his thumb and lowers his head, hovering over my lips. "I'm glad you came."

Some invisible thread pulls me up on my toes, straining to close the tiny bit of space left between our lips. Mere millimeters from his mouth, I say, "So am I."

He grips my nape and slams our lips together. This is no uncertain kiss or tentative touch. Naz plunges his tongue into my mouth, licking at me with possessive sweeps, sliding his hands over my shoulders and molding my back with his palms. His hands pause at the cinch of my waist, at the swell of my hips.

"I want to touch your ass," he says, his voice low and hoarse against my lips.

Breathless at his words, at the thought, I laugh. "Do you always ask first?"

"It feels like I should...with you." His hands tighten at my waist. "It's like...I've known you a long time, but not really. And I've kissed you before, touched you before, but it feels like that was a different world. Like maybe we're different people now."

"The person I am now wants you to touch my ass." I slide my hand down his stomach, over the taut muscles evident even through his shirt until I reach the dense curve of his butt. "As long as you don't expect me to ask before I touch yours."

His lids hang heavy over a hunter's gaze. If I'm his prey, he may not realize it, but he's caught me. Any reservation and every hesitation I had about coming and being with him, if only for two weeks, melts beneath the steam rising between us. He takes my ass in two big handfuls and squeezes, maintaining eye contact. The tight squeeze sends a jolt straight to my core, and I slide my hands up over mountainous shoulders, linking my hands behind his neck. I've never been a shy bitch. Neevah once joked that raunchy was my middle name and bold was my first. I may not be able to keep him, but I can have him for now—can temporarily block out the one huge reason this can't go beyond two weeks on the high seas.

"I've thought about you, too," I confess, the words so low I'm not sure at first I said them aloud.

"What did you think about?"

I trail my fingers back down his chest and place my hands over his where they still rest on my ass. "I was thinking about these hands. These fingers."

"What about them?" His eyes darken, and the incongruously long lashes lower to half-mast.

I tip up on my toes and draw his ear down so I can reach. "How they'd feel inside me."

I lower to my feet, pull back to watch his response. One corner of his wide, full mouth quirks up, but there's no laughter in his eyes. Only lust and need.

"You came all this way," he murmurs, gliding his hands over the curve of my ass to the hem of the loose, short dress I traveled in. "Shame for you not to find out."

"I agree. It would be—"

My words die a quick death on a harsh breath when the blunt tips of his fingers skim the skin inside my thighs. He charts a steady path toward my panties and, without hesitation, pushes them aside and strokes one rough finger over my clit.

"Jesus," I gasp, closing my eyes and dropping my head to his chest.

His breath mists the skin at my temple as he rubs slowly, adding pressure before urging my legs a little wider and inserting three fingers. My thoughts scatter. I've had dicks smaller than these three fingers. He pushes in and out, in and out, using the other hand to lift my chin and force the intimacy of our eyes connecting.

"Do they feel like you thought they would?" he asks.

I try to answer, but his thumb caresses my clit while his fingers are still occupied with burning me from the inside out.

"Y-yes," I stutter. "Better."

Words leave us, and the only sound is the sloppy wet mess he's making between my legs as he works me over. I go limp against him and grip his forearm so I can keep standing. My hips pump in rhythm with his fingers, and short, sharp breaths saw over my lips the closer I get. I'm at the precipice, about to fall over and into the orgasm of a lifetime. I can *feel* it. Sensation zings down my spine. The muscles in my stomach contract, preparing for release.

And then he stops.

"No!" The word erupts from me before I consider decorum or patience or any other virtue. "I'm close. I'm—"

"Not coming yet." His fingers leave me, and I want to sob. I want to punch him in the face for denying me. "You know what *I've* been thinking about, Kira?"

I glare up at him, ignoring the flutters winging in my belly from the way he shortens my name. "What?"

Extracting his fingers from between my legs, he holds my stare, bringing his hand up between us. "How you taste."

He shoves the wet, shiny fingers into his mouth, and I'll be damned if it isn't as sexy as him fingering me. It affects me that profoundly, seeing him lick his fingers clean and close his eyes like he's savoring a rare dish. He lifts his fingers to his nose, gathering my essence in on a ragged breath.

"I want your scent on me all night," he says, reaching down between us, under my dress, to caress the edge of my panties. "And don't you change these. I want you wearing them through dinner and thinking about how I didn't let you come."

"But you will tonight?" I ask, hating that I can't bite the question back, but *damn,* I need it now. He knows I do.

"If you're a good girl." He chuckles, starting to pull away, but I reach between us and seize his erection, hard and long, into my hands through the expensive material of his pants. God, this man could bust me open. My thighs clench in anticipation.

"And you don't touch this dick." I lean into him, rasping out my own terms, never letting his eyes go. "Don't you dare jerk off before dinner. Don't adjust it. Don't hide it. I want everyone to know what I do to you."

He pulls my panties by the edge and releases them, letting them pop against my pussy. Even that tiny contact makes me clench. Makes that aching, needing hole clamp around air, seeking him. He could have me now before dinner. We could leave his friends on the upper deck waiting while he fucks me in the position of his choice. The knowledge simmers between us, and the muscle in his jaw flexes as his famous discipline kicks in. He doesn't reply but rests one hand at my hip, taps my butt, and drops a kiss at my temple before he goes, closing the door with a controlled snick behind him.

Chapter Nine
Takira

I'm debating between two dresses for dinner—which, according to what Lotus told me on the flight here, will be a pretty snazzy affair this first night—when my cell phone rings in my purse. I grab it and continue my perusal of the closet.

"Neevah! Hey, honey. How's Iceland?"

"So gorgeous. We have to come back together."

"Well, this time it's just you and Canon, which is exactly how it should be now that the movie has wrapped. Girl, everyone, and I do mean everyone, is so excited for *Dessi Blue.*"

"I know! We get asked about it everywhere we go. Now that we've locked screen, Canon can finally relax some."

"And I hope he's making you relax, too." I try to keep my voice worry-free, though Neevah's health scares during shooting probably shaved a couple of years off my life.

"My man is taking good care of me," she assures.

"He better. Let him know he'll have me to deal with if you come home wore out."

"You just worry about getting *wore out* on that boat for the next two weeks. You there yet?"

Of course, I told Neevah about Naz's invitation and our past and the sexual tension so thick you could cut it with a pair of shears. Over the phone, I waffled on whether or not to accept Lotus's invitation and go on the cruise. My best friend was pro-go, but that's probably because Neevah's so happy with her man, she wants me to find someone, too.

"I'm here, yeah," I answer, still studying my two wardrobe options—a slinky pantsuit and a slinky dress. Either way, it'll be slinky. "Getting ready for dinner."

"How is it?" Neevah asks, barely disguised excitement in her voice.

"The yacht is huge, and everything is top tier."

"Yeah, yeah, yeah. Boat nice. Got it, but what about *him*? How is he?"

"Dangerous." I flop down onto the bed and stare up at the ceiling. "He kisses like a god and finger-fucks me like I'm his whore."

"Love that for you. I think the way to your heart will ultimately run straight through that pussy." Neevah cackles. "But why is that dangerous?"

"I told you how my brother is about him. Cliff just got better. I can't do that to him. Or at least, he can't find out what I'm doing. I'm giving in to this for two weeks, and then it's over. It's a fling."

"What if Naz doesn't want it to stop at the end of two weeks? What if *you* don't? Do you just sacrifice your happiness because of your brother's misplaced bitterness?"

"No." I close my eyes and release a troubled sigh. "I'll figure it out. I just want... I *need* this, Neeve."

In the silence between us, all the disappointments I've experienced over the years convene.

"You know the hell dating has been for me." I toy with a braid that slipped from my top knot. "Tinder disasters, blind dates, unsatisfying hook-ups, wannabe sugar daddies."

"Whew, chile. If one more old man tries to pay your rent."

"One day I'mma take it. Just lemme get tired of paying my own way. RIP to my feminism," I chuckle.

"Remember that last one offered you his 'vintage classic,' as he called it?"

"But why was it a Cutlass Supreme?" I pull my knees up to my chest and roll to my side, shaking with laughter.

There's nobody I'd rather laugh with than Neevah. We've been together a long time. Roommates in New York when we were both scraping and scratching to make it. We've supported each other through every tiny break and vowed that when the big one came, we'd bring the other up, too.

And that's exactly what Neevah did when she was cast in *Dessi Blue*. It changed both our lives. There's no one I trust more.

"Neeve, I've never wanted anyone like this," I whisper, the confession slipping out before I can stop it. "I hadn't been on the ship an hour and this man was knuckle-deep in me." I sit up straight for emphasis, even though she cannot see me. "Inside me, Neeve, and he could've gotten it.

Day one."

"I mean, half the Tinder first dates we know end in sex. How would that be any different?"

"Because *he's* different, and I have a feeling it won't be just sex." My shoulders slump with the truth, under the weight of that statement. "That with him, it could never be."

"I know that feeling well," Neevah says on a contented sigh. "You don't ignore that, even if it feels fast or impossible. If it's real, you find a way, but you'll never know if you don't try."

"But Cliff—"

"Is a grown-ass man," Neevah snaps with uncharacteristic sharpness. "You know I feel for all he's gone through. Who flew with you to Houston when he OD'd?"

"You did."

"And I would again in a heartbeat. You know there's nothing I wouldn't do for you. You're closer to me than my own sister."

"Girl, that Terry is a low bar," I chuff out an exasperated breath because I wanted to throw hands more than once with that sister of hers.

"No lies detected there, but she's getting better and working on herself. My point is, your happiness means as much to me as my own, and I'll fight anybody standing in the way of you being happy. Even your own brother, especially when his disapproval of Naz is so twisted. That boy needs therapy, not enabling."

"You're right." I nod. "Janice and I have both been trying to get him to talk to someone. He's an addict. He has a sponsor, but that's not enough. There's a lot he needs to work through."

"And I don't want you leaving something special on the table because Cliff hasn't worked through his shit yet. Don't hold back these two weeks. See if this could be anything and deal with Cliff later. Your very own fairy tale."

"A modern one. Boy meets girl. Girl gets flown out. Girl gets spoiled and bent over."

"Oh, we are here for Black girls getting spoiled and bent over."

"And do!" I let my laughter rise and fall before going on softly. "Thank you, Neeve. I love you, girl."

"Neevah." I hear Canon's deep rumbling voice through the phone. "Baby, we're late."

"And we know how obsessive your man is about time," I say dryly. "Tell him I said hey."

"Takira says hey," she purrs, a smile in her voice I only hear when

Canon is around.

"Hey, Takira," he calls. "You're making us late."

"You know how he gets." Neevah laughs. "I better go."

"Girl, bye."

"Keep me posted," she says before we hang up.

I perch on the edge of the bed for a moment, absorbing the almost undetectable motion of gentle waves lapping at the sides of the yacht. I steep in the cool opulence of this cabin. My stomach growls at the promise of the world-class menu the chef detailed when we first boarded.

Girl gets flown out. Girl gets spoilt. Girl gets bent over.

"In that order," I murmur, crossing to the closet to rub the silky material of the dress between my fingers. Naz really laid the gauntlet down.

Don't take off these panties. You don't get to come.

He thinks he can keep me riled up all night?

I strip out of the dress I traveled in and carefully slip the panties off, setting them to the side to study myself in the mirror propped up against the wall. I work out on the regular, so I'm fit, but not skinny by any means. I don't want to lose my thickness. My body is a conduit for pleasure, so I love it. One breast slightly bigger than the other. Fine lines at my hips. Little jiggle to my jam and a touch of dimples on my thighs. I'll take it all exactly as it is, and I take care of it. I glance at the juncture of my thighs, freshly waxed and ready.

"You think you got me caught up, Naz?" I wrinkle my nose at my mischievous expression in the mirror. "I got a few tricks for you."

Chapter Ten

Naz

"Where's this new girlfriend of yours?" my agent Banner asks, nibbling on a piece of skewered grilled chicken.

"She's not my girlfriend." I take a long draw of the whiskey I've been nursing off and on ever since I left Takira's cabin.

"Hmmmmph." Banner settles into the overstuffed cushions of the couch built into the wall and lining the room. A massive, beautifully set table sparkling with crystal and silverware holds court at the center of the dining room. The first to arrive, Banner and I are grazing on gourmet appetizers and sipping from the insanely well-stocked cellar's offerings. Jared had a last-minute call, but he should be joining us soon. In the meantime, I assume Banner will grill me.

"You know what I call you behind your back?" Banner asks, skirting up one dark brow.

"Won't telling me defeat the purpose of it being behind my back?" I lean into the cushions beside her.

"I'll find something else to keep from you." Her pretty face lights with a secret smile. Tonight, her abundance of dark hair spills around her shoulders. "I call you Kenan 2.0."

"I'll take that as a compliment."

"You should, but the reason I call you that is because, like Kenan, you're disciplined, calculating, careful."

"Sounds boring."

"Until you're not," she says, wagging a finger. "On the rare occasion you do something completely out of character and unexpected, I like to know why. This girl you had Lotus invite—"

"Takira."

"She's unexpected. Takira Fletcher. Does makeup and hair for a living. Originally from Houston. Went to cosmetology school after graduating from high school. Lived in Atlanta briefly before relocating to New York. Recently moved with her best friend Neevah Saint to work on Canon Holt's new biopic, *Dessi Blue*. Member of The Make-Up Artists and Hairstylist Guild since—"

"Banner," I interrupt, my tone shaded with a small warning. "What do you want to know?"

"I've checked her Tinder profile." Banner pulls out her phone. "LinkedIn. IMDb."

"Banner."

"She's clean as a whistle on the things that matter. Criminal record. Credit score."

"Jesus." I take another sip of my drink. "Is that really necessary?"

"I take care of my guys." The soft curve of Banner's mouth levels out. "I've seen too many of my players get played. So new girl shows up out of nowhere, I dig. I do the due diligence sometimes men forget when they find a nice fresh piece of ass."

"She's not..." I sigh and pinch the bridge of my nose. "It's not like that."

"She seems perfectly wonderful based on what I've learned."

"She is." I look up to meet her eyes. "I like her, Banner. And she's not out of nowhere. I met her in high school."

"I know that, too. I mean, I figured, since you played ball with her brother at St. Cat's." She laughs at the narrow-eyed look I use to search her face. "That wasn't a hard connection to make."

"Well then, you know we met when we were eighteen years old, so this is more getting reacquainted."

"Just be careful." She holds up a hand to stem the words poised on my lips. "I can take care of your career, your endorsements, your money, even your reputation to a degree. I can't take care of your heart, though, and I don't want to see you hurt." She squeezes my hand, affection in her dark eyes. "Ever."

I know how fortunate I am that Banner signed me straight out of college. She handles my business, but she cares.

"What's this?" she asks, lifting some shrimp wrapped in dough from the hors d'oeuvres plate.

A group enters the dining room in a chorus of laughter and raised voices. I glance up to find Kenan, Lotus, Iris, August, and Jared approaching.

"Ban!" Jared walks over swiftly and snatches the shrimp from her fingers, drawing a startled yelp out of her. "You can't have shellfish."

A loaded silence gathers in the room as we wait for the inevitable.

"Why can't she have shellfish?" Iris asks, drawing the question out.

"Yeah." Lotus frowns. "I know you're not allergic, so are you…?"

Realization dawns on the cousins' faces almost at the same time. Kenan, August, and I all seem to find something else to look at, careful not to reveal that we already know. Banner's lips part like she's about to explain when she seems to notice our strategically averted gazes and studied silence.

"Jared Foster!" Hands on hips, she turns on her husband. "You told."

"I didn't mean to." Jared pops the shrimp in his mouth. "Fuck. I'm sorry. I mean, it's not a secret you can keep for long anyway. What's the point?"

Banner rolls her eyes, surrendering to a happy laugh and accepting the ensuing squeals and questions from Iris and Lotus. Under the cover of all the excitement, no one notices Takira slip through the dining room doors.

No one except me.

I leave the group and cross over to her. My steps literally falter for a second when I see what she's wearing. Or *not* wearing. The silvery-white halter dress ties at her nape with fragile straps and dips low in the front, nearly to her belly button, contrasting against the gleaming curves of her shoulders and breasts, baring her arms. It clings to her hips and ass but floats around her thighs in frothy layers. When she walks a little ahead of me, the dress is so low the small of her back is visible.

Is she even wearing underwear?

She looks fantastic. Anticipation swells inside me at the thought of introducing her to my friends. I grab Takira's wrist and pull her close, leaning down to whisper in her ear, "You look amazing."

She slants an innocent look up at me. Her dress may not be subtle, but her makeup is. A smoky eye shadow and the slightest tilt of a cat eye at the corners. Nude lipstick and her braids styled into an elaborate updo studded with crystals.

"I was worried you wouldn't approve," she says with a small pout.

"Why not? You look gorgeous."

"Well, I know you wanted me to wear these," she says, shoving a ball of silk into my hand and closing my fingers around it. "And this dress doesn't allow for panties."

"Shit, Kira." I shove the panties into the pockets of my slacks.

I'm not sure which part makes my dick hardest—her slightly damp panties in my pocket, the sexy-as-fuck dress that barely covers her butt cleavage, or the fact that she just told me her pussy is bare under there.

"Come on." She turns her back on the room, grinning up at me and tugging my hand where I still grasp her wrist. "Aren't you gonna introduce me to your friends?"

Chapter Eleven
Takira

My head is buzzing, and I haven't even had a drop of liquor. My brain is overloaded with names and connections and relationships. When Lotus invited me on this trip, she said it would be a few close friends, which is technically true. There are just so many powerful personalities in one room. Rarely do I feel intimidated. I move in some rarefied circles from time to time in my line of work and rub up against entertainment industry elite, but everyone here is at the top of their game somehow.

Banner and Jared, a power couple, two elite sports agents.

Kenan and Lotus, obviously. Her, one of the buzziest names in fashion; him, a basketball legend, guaranteed first-round Hall of Famer with business enterprises all over the world.

August and Iris. Him, a franchise player, one of the best in the League right now. Apparently Iris is becoming a force in her own right, handling huge accounts with their sports agency, Elevation.

Adding to the bad-assery, Lotus's close friends and business partners Billie and Yari are here with their boyfriends. Kenan's sister Kenya, a WNBA player, is here with her new wife, Jade, who apparently is a songwriter and producer and cousin to Grip, one of the greatest lyricists of our generation.

So, yeah. It's a lot. *They're* a lot.

The food was fantastic. The conversation—stimulating, intelligent, hilarious. The best time I've had over a meal in…maybe ever. Naz's friends are incredible, and it's obvious he cares about them as much as they care about me. They were accepting and kind, though *extremely* curious. I wouldn't get this many questions on *Jeopardy*.

"I need a drink," I tell Naz, glancing around the emptying dining room.

"Then let's get you one." He walks us over to the bar, and I ask the bartender to surprise me. I don't particularly care what I drink right now, as long as it takes this edge off.

"Didn't want to drink much during dinner," I tell Naz. "I had to keep a clear head for the inquisition."

"Ugh." He groans but grins. "My friends are nosy."

"They probably just want to make sure I'm not a ball bunny, or whatever you guys call those women who wait in the tunnel offering you ass after games." I nudge him with my shoulder while the bartender prepares my drink.

"Ball bunnies?" He lifts both brows.

"Oh, please. A man fine as you? I'm sure you get your share."

"You think I'm attractive?"

I tip up to whisper in his ear, "Would my panties be in your pocket if I didn't?"

"Here you go," the bartender says, offering me an amber-colored drink before Naz has the chance to respond with anything other than a heated stare.

"This is delicious," I say after a sip. "What is it?"

"It's a Genoa." He offers Naz one, too. "Mediterranean drink in honor of our journey. Gin, grappa, sambuca, dry vermouth with an olive. Glad you like it."

"You guys keeping all the good liquor to yourselves?" Kenya asks, rising from the dining room table.

She looks like a softer version of Kenan, tall and lean with locs hanging past her shoulders. She and Jade are newlyweds and have been stuck to each other's sides all night. It's sweet how they're even now holding hands...with twined fingers!

"You've had enough," Jade mumbles as they cross the room to us. "You know how your ass gets."

"Once! You cry once after a bottle of tequila," Kenya laughs. "And your wife never lets you live it down."

"Nah." Jade runs a hand over her neat cornrows. "It's also that jet lag I'm worried about. Gin and jet lag—not a good look for you."

"What we need is some fresh air," Kenya says. "It'll clear my head. Everybody's up on deck. You guys coming?"

The look Naz rolls over me is molten, and even my fast tail feels self-conscious under it.

"I think they want to be alone," Kenya says, her voice sing-song and teasing.

"No, we'll come," I say, quirking one brow in challenge. He thought he could edge me? See how he likes being put on hold.

"Sure," Naz agrees instantly, mocking me with a toast of his Genoa.

When we get up to the deck, I'm glad we came. The whole group is up here, and the lights strung along the ship glow, casting a romantic spell over everyone. With the breeze whipping dresses and hair and cooling heated cheeks, we all line up at the rail and lean into the sea spray. Under moonlight, we sip our drinks, weaving in and out of conversations with each other and with our partners. It's a perfect evening, but like Jada suggested, jet lag starts kicking in, and after an hour, I slump my back against Naz's wide chest, barely able to stand.

"You're tired," he whispers, his lips brushing the sensitive skin at my throat.

"Maybe a little bit," I sleep-slur, clutching the powerful forearms wrapped around my waist.

"Hey, guys," he calls to his friends—some still at the rail, some lying on the lounge chairs together by now. "This one's exhausted and jet lagged. I'mma take her to her room."

"See you tomorrow," Iris says, standing and crossing over to us. "We're so glad you're here."

"Yeah." Lo walks up beside us, tugging Kenan behind her. "Next time, you come and leave Naz at home."

"Whatever," Naz says, shaking his head. "We out."

We board the elevator to take us to the lower deck where our cabins are located. I lean against one wall, and he leans against the other, watching me, unsmiling. My heart picks up speed at the intensity of his stare. When the elevator dings, signaling we've reached our floor, he pulls my panties out of his pocket and holds them up. "You have to answer for these."

"What?"

"You think you can keep me hard all night without some form of retribution?"

"I don't—"

The elevator doors open, and he gently pushes me through them and into the small waiting area.

"Run," he says, that predator's glaze over his eyes.

It takes half a second for my flight instinct to kick in. I take off down the corridor, glad I've been wearing heels my whole life, and I run in them as easily as I do barefoot.

"Naz!" I screech, laughing, adrenaline pumping as his heavy footsteps gain on me. I know it's a game, but the heat I just saw in his eyes, the erection tenting his pants—they send danger signals to my nervous system. Even if the only danger I'm in is of getting fucked all night.

I round the corner, my room in view, when one stone-hard arm encircles my waist and snatches me up. I'm five nine and thick with it. It's not often I'm "snatched up" like I weigh nothing, but he literally carries me under his arm, and my legs dangle in the air.

"Got you," he murmurs, slowly lowering me to the floor and pressing my front to the door. "Open it."

His heat at my back, his dick pressing into me, his breath in my hair. It's so much, I mis-enter the code for the door three times before it swings open. The bedside lamp casts a faint glow over the room. The bed has been turned down, and it invites me to lower my weary body onto the cool sheets.

Still behind me, Naz splays his hand over my stomach and drifts lower, pressing into the juncture of my thighs through my dress.

"Are you really not wearing underwear?" he asks, his voice gruff and maybe a little hopeful.

I turn to face him, walking backward until my knees hit the bed, and I lie down, allowing the dress's feathery hem to spray around the tops of my thighs, barely hiding the truth between my legs. I spread just the tiniest bit for him but not enough for him to know for sure. With an impatient sound, he walks over, drags me to the edge of the bed so my legs hang over the side, and goes down on his knees. He eases the dress up the last few inches until the cool air hits my bare, wet pussy.

"Shit, Kira." A frown wrinkles the thick line of his brows. "Is that a—"

"Clit clamp," I say, widening even more so the Swarovski crystal winks at him from the shadows between my thighs. "Yeah."

He swallows audibly, his hand hovering over my naked flesh from the waist down. "You wore it for me?"

"I think I'm probably gonna get a lot more out of it than you are." I laugh. "I've been wearing it all night, so when you take it off, all the blood will rush to my clit, and it'll hurt like a motherfucker, but it will also feel incredible. So…it's for both of us really."

I've worn this before, and when men see it, they usually dive in right away, eager for something they see as illicit and novel. Not Naz. His stare locks on to the space between my legs for long moments before he runs his palms behind my knees and then up my thighs. He repeats this motion over and over again, kneading the muscles of my legs, skimming my calves, dragging his short nails over the sensitive skin of my inner thighs, all the while getting maddeningly closer, but never close enough to where I want to feel him most. My body starts to move compulsively, in synch with the pressure, with the motion of his hands, rolling under his palms. One of his fingers skims the lips of my pussy, and I jerk. My nerves are drawn tight with anticipation now, and I'd take any touch *right there.*

He lowers his face between my legs, and I stretch open for him shamelessly, as wide as my legs will go.

"Naz, please." I hate the begging in my voice, but I'm so wet and needy.

"Tell me," he says, not looking away from my pussy. "What do you want?"

My hips are pumping, and I reach behind my neck to untie the halter. My breasts spill free, and I cup one of them. His eyes snap up, and his breathing harshens as I roll my nipple.

"I *can* do this for myself, you know," I say, sliding one hand between my legs.

His big hand grasps my wrist with firm gentleness and presses it to my side on the bed. He watches my fingers tweaking my nipple, watches the tip harden and burgeon. I squeeze as much for the sensation as for his reaction, which is a tightening of his mouth. I drag my hand away from my breast and try again to reach between my legs.

"I wanna take this off." I reach for the crystal clamp.

"Don't you fucking touch it." His voice is Brillo and velvet, and the command in it makes me shiver. "I'll do it."

And then, my god, he does.

He pulls back the lips, opening me like the petals of a flower, and lowers his mouth to me.

Barely.

His tongue traces the clamp, licking and sucking in little wisps of touch.

"Oh, god, Naz," I moan. "I need you to—"

"I know, baby," he breathes over my wetness. "Let me take care of you."

With his tongue and teeth, he toys with the clamp until it pulls free of my clit. The blood flow that was suppressed all night rushes to that one point on my body in a flood of pain and pleasure. Both wash over me in waves, and I shudder as the sensations do battle in my nerve endings. Before I have the chance to decide if it hurts more than it feels good, he's there, sucking me into his mouth. Soothing the nerves and stimulating them simultaneously. With one hand, he peels me back and opens his mouth wide over me, ravenous, burying his face between my legs and making grunting, growling, *starving* noises. The pleasure is so intense, I try to slide back on the bed, to get away, but he holds me in place by my hip, never letting up or letting go.

A coil low in my belly starts unwinding, surging pleasure down my legs and clenching the muscles in my stomach. I scream. Someone said these rooms are soundproof, but I don't care. The whole group could be having tea outside my door, and there's no way I could hold back the sounds his mouth is drawing from me.

Finally, I burst, my back bowing, neck arching, hot tears rolling into my hairline, release flowing from me. He pulls my legs over his shoulders, taking my ass into his hands and spreading me open even more.

"You have to stop," I beg, pressing my heels into his back, sobs wracking my body. "It's too much."

He ignores me, his hands running up and down my thighs with reverence, and he keeps licking and sucking. My arms rest on the bed limply, and my head lolls back and forth. I've never felt this spent from oral alone. When he finally lifts his head, he smiles at me, the clit clamp held between his strong white teeth.

"You're crazy." I breathe out a chuckle, reaching up to run my hand across his hair. He's so damn beautiful. The most beautiful boy I'd ever seen has grown into a man I can't take my eyes off.

He gently rolls me onto my stomach and deals with the hidden zip at the base of my dress, then peels the silky material away from my body. He cups my ass, rubbing it, and then I feel his lips, still damp with my release, kiss one cheek and then the other. Slowly, he rolls me onto my back again and tugs me into a sitting position. Still dressed and with his dick at my eye level, he begins removing the pins from my hair. Braids spill around my shoulders. I touch his erection, and he draws a harsh breath.

"Naz, don't you want—"

"There'll be time."

"I want something for you, too, tonight."

He bends to run his hand from my breast to the soaked juncture of my thighs, slipping the rough pad of his finger over my swollen clit.

"That *was* for me." He smiles, but his eyes remain sober. "You're for me. Do you wear a hair scarf to bed?"

"Um, yeah." I nod to the bedside table where I stowed some of my things.

He brings it over and gives it to me. "Show me how you do it."

I wrap the scarf around my braids like I do every night, my hands trembling under his intense scrutiny.

"Do you wash your face?"

"Yeah," I say, standing, suddenly self-conscious that I'm naked and he's not. I walk to the bathroom, *feeling* his eyes on my back and ass and legs. In the bathroom, he grabs a washcloth from the neat stack on the counter. After wetting it with warm water, he brings it to my pussy, gently cleaning me. My breath stutters, and my heart batters my chest from the inside at his tender touch, at the thorough way he uses the wipes on the counter to remove my makeup.

What *is* this?

Once he's cleaned me up and removed my makeup, he leads me back to the bed, pulls the coverlet back, and gives me a gentle push into the coolness of the sheets.

Let me take care of you.

He said it when he was eating me out like a starved animal, but the way he's actually doing it breaks something in me. Emotion swells inside. All the searching and settling over the years feel like a distant memory under his attention. All the times I wanted to feel special and got a dick pic instead, or got called a bitch by a strange man because I didn't respond to his vulgar DM—those times fade because this was what I wanted all along.

To feel this special. This considered. This wanted and respected.

"Will you stay?" I ask, my voice low and a little shaky. The oral was fantastic, but this...this is something else.

"Do you want me to?"

Not trusting my voice with more words, I simply nod and watch as he removes his clothes, folding them neatly and placing them in a chair in the corner. His body is like a machine, but warm and gleaming and taut, his muscles seemingly rippling in places other men never even had muscles. He crawls in behind me, pulling me close. My back is pressed into his wide, smooth chest. And though I feel him semi-erect against my backside through his briefs, he makes no move. When he tucks his head into the crook of my neck and lays a kiss there, I reach behind me and cup the back of his head. There's no way two weeks will be enough. Not with this man. So many thoughts swirl in my head, and despite the jet lag and exhaustion, I'm staring into the dark unblinkingly, wondering what the hell I've gotten myself into.

"Kira," he says after a few minutes of easy silence, splaying his hand possessively over my belly. "Baby, go to sleep."

And as if my body knows something I don't, it obeys.

Chapter Twelve

Naz

I wake up alone to sunshine, fresh linen, and Takira's scent all over me.

That woman will be end of me. I'm not an asshole. I'm considerate to the women I sleep with, sure. But to defer sex altogether and only ensure their pleasure?

Defeats the purpose.

But *her* pleasure was my only purpose last night.

Glancing over to the empty spot where she should be, I drag my hands over my face. She probably thinks I have some kind of daddy-little girl thing because I basically tucked her in and put her to bed after oral.

"You did everything but read her a bedtime story."

I've never felt that way. I just wanted to take care of her—for her to feel like she was my priority. Because she was.

My dick strains against my briefs, giving me an angry *what about us* poke.

"You'll get yours when you get it," I mutter, my hand drifting down and into my underwear. I could take the edge off now, but do I really want jizz all in Takira's sheets when she comes back to bed?

Where is she?

A faint sound from the bathroom draws my attention. Is she okay? The door is ajar, so I get out of bed and walk to the bathroom to make sure she's not seasick or having any discomfort from the food last night.

"Kira?" I ask, pushing the door open a little wider and poking my head in.

"Seriously?!" she hollers from the toilet, her expression one of horror. "I'm peeing in here."

I should back out...or I could have a little fun. I lean into the doorjamb and cross my arms across my chest. "I was so far up your pussy last night I tasted your heartbeat, but you're self-conscious about me seeing you pee?"

"It's not the..." She closes her eyes and draws in a deep breath. The scarf she tied over her braids last night is askew, and it's the only scrap of material on her whole body. She collapses her long legs at the knees, I guess so I don't see what I've already seen *and* tasted. She grips the sides of the toilet, and her breasts hang freely.

"One tit is bigger than the other," she says, cocking one brow. "But I'm sure you know that by now with all the staring."

"From what I remember last night, I love them equally."

"You actually didn't bother much with my breasts."

"True. I was too preoccupied with your pussy."

"You are really, really," she says, closing her eyes briefly and biting her lip, "good at eating me out. I've only ever had oral that good with a woman. Men don't usually take that kind of time, from my experience."

I stiffen. I don't like her comparing me to anyone else. No one would, right? I'm not weirdly possessive or territorial. Nah, not me.

"What?" she asks, brows drawn together. "You have a problem with the girl thing?"

"That you're bisexual? No, as long as you're only *me-sexual* now."

"You mean for the next two weeks," she clarifies with a small smile.

"If you say so," I scoff because good luck walking away from this thing between us in two weeks. I cover the small distance from the door to the toilet.

"Naz, you cannot be in here while I'm on the toilet!"

"I promise if it was number two, I wouldn't be."

"Ewwww." She turns her head to the side, closing her eyes. "This just gets worse."

"I'll make it better." I bend to kiss her cheek and reach down to cup her breasts. She goes still and her breath hitches. I drag my thumbs over her nipples, loving how they bloom, harden under my touch. She has no idea how she affects me. On one hand, I want to keep it that way because no woman has ever had this much power over me, especially in so little time. On the other hand, I want her to know she could probably get anything she wants from me because I'd like to give it to her.

"Naz," she pants, leaning into my touch, her breasts filling my palms. "This is crazy. I'm on the toilet."

"You mentioned that." I chuckle.

There's a knock at the door, and I blow out a frustrated breath.

"I'll get it." I stride from the bathroom to the cabin door, cracking it open, poking my head out since I'm wearing only my briefs.

"Naz!" Lotus glances up at the number above the door. "I'm sorry. I could have sworn this was…"

Standing in the hall wearing tiny shorts and a crop top that shows off her baby bump, she gasps, her dark eyes widening and her mouth rounding into an O.

"This *is* Takira's room. Did you guys make sex in there?"

"Nunya. Could you not make this weird, Lo? What do you want?"

"I'm happy for you." She beams. "It's obvious you like her a lot. Like *a lot, a lot.* You watched her all through dinner. I've never seen you like this with anyone else. It's actually kind of presh."

"Uh-huh." I glance over my shoulder to make sure Takira's still in the bathroom. "Maybe lower your voice when you talk about how whipped I already am?"

"What's happening?" Banner asks, coming up beside Lotus, already dressed in her bikini and a sheer wrap. "Are we still doing jet skis?"

"Yeah." Lotus grins up at me, relishing every second of this encounter. "But I got distracted by Naz being in Takira's room."

"Awwww." Banner presses her hands over her heart. "Are you guys fucking? That is so dear. I know I had a lot of questions, but having dinner with her last night, she's a delight."

Slim arms wrap around my waist from behind, and Takira pokes her head around me at the door. I glance over my shoulder to see she's wearing a floor-length silk robe now.

"Did someone say jet skis?" Takira asks, excitement obvious in her voice.

"Yes!" Lotus claps three times. "You want to?"

"Of course." Takira steps out into the hall, leaving me still stranded and undressed with my head at the door. "I'm an island girl. I was practically born on a jet ski."

"I've never done it," Banner chimes in. "Sounds like fun."

"Never done what?" Jared asks, walking up the hall.

"Is this a yacht convention?" I mutter.

"Never jet skied," Banner replies, tucking into his side under his arm and tipping her face up for a kiss.

"Not sure you should." Jared frowns. "Did the doctor clear that?"

"I think riding you is more rigorous than riding a jet ski," Banner parries.

A wicked grin spreads over Jared's face. "Then you should be fine."

He flicks a glance at Takira and then at me.

"Speaking of last night's sex," Jared drawls. "Did I interrupt a walk of shame?"

"Could y'all just go?" I nearly shout. "Yes to jet skis. Now leave."

"All right, all right," Lotus mumbles. "We're just having fun."

"So yes to jet skis?" Kenan asks, walking up the hall. "Breakfast is ready, by the way."

His gaze drifts over the small group clustered outside the cabin door and then to me still tucked behind it.

"Damn, y'all." Kenan tsks, continuing past them. "Give them some privacy."

"Thank you," I say. "I knew I could count on you at least."

"How does it feel being the mature one in the group, Kenan?" Lotus yells, laughing at his back. "That's why you turning forty!"

He doesn't break stride but raises his middle finger in the air, a deep chuckle accompanying him down the hall.

"I guess we *should* eat," Jared says, turning to leave. "See you at breakfast. Come on, Ban."

She takes Jared's hand and starts down the hall but sends me a wink over her shoulder.

"Okay, so breakfast up on deck and jet skis in an hour," Lotus says. "Sound good?"

"Sounds great," Takira says. "And thank you again for including me. This is such a great trip, and everyone's so nice."

"I'm glad you're here," Lotus says. "And I really would like to pick your brain about the Carnival campaign for next summer."

"Would love that."

"Okay, well, I should let you go before Naz's head explodes," Lotus says wryly. "See you up top."

Takira comes back into the room, shutting the door behind her. Her robe gapes open enough for me to see the top curves of her breasts, and my mouth waters because I haven't tasted them yet. I'm yanked from my own salacious thoughts by Takira's hand on my dick through my briefs.

"Is she right?" Takira asks, her touch firm, her eyes fixed on mine. "Is your *head* about to explode?"

I grip her throat, lifting her chin with my thumb. "If you keep pulling on it like that, hell yeah."

She laughs, leaning into me, her naked breasts meeting my bare chest. I slide one hand under her robe, trailing over her plump ass.

A loud pounding on the door breaks the spell our bodies are weaving over us.

"Come to breakfast, lovebirds!" August yells through the door. "You can do that stuff later. Apparently, we're going jet skiing."

An exasperated sigh flows out of me, but Takira steps away, chuckling and pulling her robe tightly around her as she walks back to the bathroom.

"Later," she says over one silk-covered shoulder. "I promise."

Chapter Thirteen
Takira

It's actually been a long time since I was on a jet ski, so today was amazing. Though my family left Trinidad shortly after I was born and moved to Houston, I still consider the island my home. We visit family there often, and every time I chase the waves, extend my arms to the sky, and surrender to the wind. It never feels like a visit, but like a reunion with the elements that formed me.

Today it's a Mediterranean breeze wafting over my face, not a Caribbean sigh. And the blue sky and fluffy clouds above are hung over Capri, not my beloved Tobago, but I still felt that invigoration that only sand and sea ever stir in me. The sea spray on my face and water sloshing onto my legs. Naz laughing at my back, his sinewed arms cradling me while we rode the waves together. Having him warm and hard behind me was my favorite part of the day.

And, boy, was he hard.

After last night, how blue are that man's balls?

I want to give him some relief. Selfishly, I want to suck his dick. It's not fair he knows how I taste and I'm still over here wondering. In our bathing suits, we're headed below deck, walking down the narrow stairwell leading to our rooms. I stop, turning abruptly to face Naz. His hard body slams into me, and my nipples pebble against his chest.

"Oh, sorry," he says. "I didn't mean to—"

He's one step above me, and I slowly lower to my knees on the step below.

"Um, what…" Confusion pinches his dark brows together. "What's happening right now?"

"Oh, it's even worse than I thought." I shake my head in mock despair. "You don't even know when you're about to get a blow job."

He glances up the stairwell behind him. "Here? Now?"

My fingers, nimble and sure, work at the lacing of his trunks.

"Half the group went ashore to shop," I remind him. "Half of them are still swimming or on the jet skis. And Jared and Banner are in their cabin, probably having wild sex."

"Yeah," he mutters absently, eyes fixed on me as I slide his trunks down over his powerful thighs. "Those hormones are intense."

"Damn, Naz." I feast my eyes on his dick, proud and jutting out. "This is a lot. I may choke." I grin up at him sweetly. "A girl can hope."

"Maybe we should go——"

"No one's gonna see," I reassure him, taking his dick in hand and laughing when he makes a strangled sound. "Besides, the threat of getting caught makes it better."

I glance up at him, infusing my eyes with all the lust coursing through my body.

"But you should know, if someone comes, I won't stop. I don't give a damn if someone sees me sucking you off." I chuckle and undo the straps of my bikini top so my breasts spill out. "They can enjoy the show."

It's not true, but the *thought* of it being true gets his dick even harder in my hands, and I grin, licking my lips for him. "You like that, don't you? Well, there's something you should know before we start."

"What?" he asks, glancing over his shoulder again.

I run my lips over the swollen tip, sucking the pre-cum already leaking there like he's my personal straw. "I give really good head."

I take him in my mouth all the way, letting him sink just a little into my throat.

Damn, he's big.

My gag reflex does not want to let me be great, kicking in right away, so I pull back some and swirl my tongue around the head. I grip the base, sliding my hand, which feels so small and barely closes around him, up and down his rigid length. Looking up at him, catching and holding his eyes, I slide my mouth all the way down and off, letting him pop out so I can dip my head to his balls. They're smooth and still cool from the sea. When I take one into my mouth and cup the other, he groans. His eyes are squeezed shut, and his fist is pressed to the stairwell wall. I switch balls, taking the other into my mouth and rolling the other, still wet from my attention, in my hand.

"Dammit, Kira," he growls, his brows furrowed. "You better not fucking stop."

I take his dick back into my mouth, grinning at the command all over his face and in the deep rumble of his voice. I drop my jaw and slowly take him down as far as I can. Letting the walls of my throat close around him, I force myself to swallow, the muscles clenching around him.

"Fuuuuuuuuck," he groans, banging the wall.

I bob my head, breathing through my nose when he goes deeper. I squeeze my thumb to help squelch the gag reflex. I read somewhere that helps. Not sure if it's true, but with a dick this big, it's worth a try. I keep rolling one ball in my other hand. I see when he loses himself completely—when the risk of discovery, the concern that he would hurt me, everything is consumed by the need and the passion. He takes my head between his two massive hands, holding me exactly like he wants, and fucks my mouth relentlessly. I choke, saliva spilling from the sides of my mouth, tears blurring my vision, but I don't protest. I'm riveted by the aching pleasure on his handsome face. You could not pry this man's dick from my mouth right now. Not because of him, but because of me. I am the vessel of his mindless bliss, and it feels like a privilege. A man who's so careful, so calculating—losing himself in me.

I'm his undoing.

His gasping, panting, shouting undoing.

"I'm coming," he moans. "If you want me to—"

"Swallow," I mumble around his dick. Not sure if he understands because he pulls out.

"I said I'll swallow, Naz," I rasp, my throat literally aching from how hard he fucked it.

"I want to come on your face," he gasps, his voice a dark rumble as he searches my expression. It's as if he's discovering something about himself in the depths of my eyes.

"Then come on my face," I tell him, not hesitating. "Whatever pleases you will please me, Naz."

And it does. As thick streams of his cum splatter my face, I lick my lips, savoring the salty flavor of him. Groaning my deepest pleasure as he dips to spread it over my throat and shoulders. It sluices between my breasts and anoints my nipples. The whole time, my fingers are busy in my bikini bottom, rubbing my clit and burrowing my fingers inside myself. I can barely stand on my knees when the orgasm hits. It's like a volcano, him spewing all over me, and me exploding within. I tip my head back, dry sobs ripping from my throat.

"You are so fucking beautiful like this," he groans, gripping my hair to tip my head back so our eyes lock. He places his dick at my mouth and, like an artist, paints the bow with the wet, salty tip.

"Thank you," I choke out, and I mean it.

Some might feel degraded on their knees where anyone could walk by and see him coating me with his release. My breasts are bared to him, and my face, throat, and torso are soaked in long ribbons of his cum. I may be on my knees, but as he looks at me with something approaching awe and uses his finger to scrawl the three letters of his name in the cum on my chest, I feel lifted. I'm floating as the perfectly chiseled lines of his face fold into an agony of need. His composure lies in tatters at my feet.

I'm a fucking goddess. And this was an act of worship.

Chapter Fourteen

Naz

"You made this mess." Takira laughs up at me from the step below. "You have to clean it."

I still haven't caught my breath. Hell, I'm not sure I've even breathed since she dropped to her knees and told me she gives great head.

For the record, she does.

My brain must still be on the floor because I'm not even processing the words she's saying. I fucked her mouth hard. I lost control. Cupping her face, with my thumb I trace her lips, swollen and still shiny from my release.

"Come on." She turns her head to kiss my palm and stands. "I'm sticky."

She continues down the steps, re-tying her bikini top as she goes. "Shower?" she asks, smiling at me over her shoulder.

"Uh…" I'm still planted on the steps, scraping shreds of my soul off the walls. "Yeah. Sure."

She punches in the code to her cabin, and I follow behind her. Stripping out of her bikini, not even sparing me a glance, she tosses it into a hamper at the bathroom door. She's completely free and unselfconscious. I've never been with a woman like her.

"You coming?" she asks, disappearing into the bathroom.

I shake myself and move on legs that still feel wobbly. That woman sucked the life out of me, but also awoke some of the darkest urges I didn't even know lurked under the surface.

I want to come on your face?

Where did that come from? She probably thinks I'm…

No, she doesn't. Takira is the most uninhibited, non-judgmental person I've ever met. I'm someone who likes to strategize and calculate every move, but with her, I'm different. I should have known when I stepped out of character and asked Lo to invite her that Takira would affect me this way. That because of her, I would surprise myself.

And yet I'm still reeling and unprepared.

When I enter the bathroom, she's naked and testing the water with her fingers. She's tall and thick, rounded and juicy. Her ass and breasts jiggle when she moves. Even the tiny striations at her hips turn me on because they're on *her*. There's something about a woman who's so comfortable in her skin with what some would consider flaws. It's powerful.

She steps into the shower, and I strip off my trunks to follow. When she reaches for her sponge, I take it from her fingers.

"I'll wash you."

Even though she teased that I would have to clean up the mess I made, I can tell by the surprise on her face she didn't think I intended to. After a brief hesitation, she nods. I turn her into the steam of water, watching all evidence that I came all over her in the stairwell wash away. Her breasts are round and proud, and as I stare, her nipples swell.

"More washing." She laughs. "Less gawking."

I angle a smile at her and squeeze soap onto the sponge, working a lather into her taut brown skin. Her breath hitches when I wash her breasts, taking my time to lift their weight and clean the soft undersides, then I linger on her nipples, bend to take them, wet and turgid, into my mouth. I go down on my knees and drag the sponge over her legs, behind her knees. I wash her feet, paying special attention to the graceful arch. Her toes twitch.

"Ticklish?" I chuckle.

"Something like that." She runs a hand over my hair and looks down at me, affection softening the bold lines of her face. "That night at my house, on the roof, I thought you were the most beautiful boy I'd ever seen. I knew you'd grow up to be a beautiful man, Naz, but I had no idea."

Hearing her refer to our past, however brief it was, does something to me. My chest tightens, and I swallow deeply. We only had one night, but it's one I've never forgotten. *She* is the one I've never forgotten.

"I feel cheated," I admit, gently pushing her to the bench in the shower.

"Why?"

"What if we could have had this all along? What if we'd gotten to see *then* where this could go?"

"It's the past," she says, caressing the nape of my neck.

I push her legs open and sit back on my heels, studying her pretty pussy. No one will take this—her—away from me again. My will hardens, and I grit my teeth.

Fuck two weeks.

When I open her up, her clit still seems a little swollen. Not sure if it's from last night's clit clamp or arousal. She tasted so good. I loved waking up, smelling her all around me, all over me. I hitch one of her thighs over my shoulder and French kiss her slit, pulling the nub of nerves into my mouth.

"Ooooh, Naz, yes," she moans, undulating into my kiss. "That's it."

In seconds, I'm devouring her, barely cognizant of her cries. She's slick with water and her own essence. Her scent mixes with the bodywash, and it's heady and intoxicating. She digs one hand into my scalp and the other into my shoulder while she rides it out, stiffening with her orgasm and slumping into the wall.

When I look up, her pupils are blown wide with lust and satisfaction. Her mouth hangs open, staccato breaths forced from her heaving chest. Our eyes lock, and for long seconds, neither of us says anything. Our connection, even though we haven't fully consummated it, is incredibly sexual, but it's also intimate. Every hot touch is tender and caring, even the ones that carry a sting of pain like her nails digging into my arm. *Worth it.*

She stands, taking my hand and pulling me to my feet. With a gentle shove to my shoulder, she pushes me down to the bench where she was just seated.

"Stay here," she says, her voice hushed, husky. "I'll be right back."

She's only gone seconds, and when she returns, it's with a gold foil square. My eyes zip to her face. She holds it up, and for once, her smile carries a trace of uncertainty.

"I mean…" She slides her eyes to the mosaic tiles of the shower. "If you want to."

I reach for her, grab her by the ass, and pull her toward me to stand between my long legs spread where I'm seated on the bench.

"I want," I mutter, my voice so deep and low I barely recognize it. "I want everything you have, Kira."

And I don't just mean her body. We've only been back in each other's lives for such a short time, and we only had one night years ago, but I want everything from this woman. Her secrets, her fears, her hopes, and ambitions. I want to see where we could go.

She eases her spread thighs over mine, and my legs are so long and so much bigger than hers, it stretches her wide open. Compared to me, she's small, and it makes me want to be careful. As strong as she is, the last thing I would ever want to do is hurt her.

"Hey." I take her jaw into my hand and wait for her to look at me. "I want you to know this is important to me. You're important to me, Kira."

She blinks, surprise and pleasure darkening her beautiful eyes. "For me, too," she says.

I lean in, cupping her head and kissing her, urging her lips open so I can taste her again. Her sweetness mixes with the saltiness of my cum on her tongue, and I growl. Tasting myself on her unleashes a primal urge inside me, and I grip her butt in my hands, bringing her close to hover over my stiff dick.

"Whoa, whoa, whoa, sir." She grins, holding up the condom again. "What you not gonna do is hit it raw the first time. Let's wrap this right on up. This is the biggest condom I have. I hope it fits."

We both laugh as she slides the condom over my length with fingers that tremble the slightest bit. When it's fitted over me, our laughter dissipates. Her expression sobers, and she leans forward, grips my nape, and rains kisses over my nose, my cheekbones, my chin. I catch her mouth with mine, groaning when she sucks my tongue inside, exploring the roof of my mouth. Finally, she presses her forehead to mine, bracing her arms on my shoulders to lift and then sink down onto me.

A shared breath whooshes from us both as she takes as much as she can.

"Fuck, Naz." She grimaces.

I look between us, almost losing my mind at seeing myself halfway in and her body stretched around me.

"How much more?" she asks, breathless.

"You can do it," I murmur, squeezing both cheeks of her ass and running my hands up her back. "I know you can take it all."

"Just gimme a sec," she pants, easing down another inch or so.

"Shit!" The word explodes from me as her tight pussy clamps around my dick, taking more of me. My mind spins and my abs clench as she moves the slightest bit, rocking her hips in tight undulations all while sliding down a little more until she's spread over me, and when I look between us, I don't see my dick at all. Her pussy has eaten me up, swallowed me whole. She lifts her chin, eyes alight with triumph and lust.

"I did it," she gasps, rocking onto me.

"You're so good." I grunt into the wet curve of her neck. "So good. I knew you could do it, baby."

I slump back into the shower wall, holding her hips as she rolls over me, the muscles of her thighs flexing as she rises and falls, her expression twisting as I screw up into her body. Her breasts bounce, and she throws her head back, bottom lip trapped between her teeth, drops of water spraying over her back and shoulders, droplets gliding down her belly to christen the place where our bodies interlock. I rub and pinch her clit, and she screams, her shoulders shaking with hoarse cries as our movements turn frenzied. Her muscles seize around me as she comes, burying her face into my neck, shaking with her release.

I stand, keeping her close, not allowing space between our bodies, and walk over to the shower wall. Pressing into her, pinning her there, I reach for her leg to anchor at my back. She's listless, still coming down, her eyes rolling back and her mouth slack. I give her no time to recover, but surge inside her.

"Oh!" Her eyes go wide. "Naz."

There's a drum in my head, in my heart. It's primitive, percussive, unrelenting, and it possesses me. I pound into her, pushing her body into a wet slide up the wall. Her legs slip on and off my ass while she tries to anchor herself.

"Is it too much?" I manage to clear my head long enough to ask, unable to even let up while I wait for her answer. I only pray that if she says it's too much, I can pull back.

She digs her nails into my neck, jerks my head toward her until her lips are at my ear.

"Harder." Her breath is hot at my throat as she locks her ankles at the base of my spine. "I wanna have trouble sitting down. Can you do that for me, Naz?"

"Jesus, Kira." I grunt, planting my feet wider, gripping her thigh so tightly I'm afraid it will bruise. "You shouldn't have said that."

I'm like a berserker who's lost the thread of time and reason, lost to a fever, to madness. Whatever beast this woman awakened in me roars out of his cage and fucks her into that wall, heedless of anything but the legs splayed and the tight opening dripping for him. He takes and takes and takes and takes. He takes until he's satisfied. He takes until she is, too.

Chapter Fifteen

Takira

I did ask for this.

I told Naz I wanted to have trouble sitting down, and for days I've been walking like I had a stick up my ass because I basically have. More like a tree trunk. I'm still getting used to him, but damn if it's not the best sex of my life. I would not change one thing, one moment, but I'm just starting to walk with no twinges of discomfort.

He's abandoned his cabin completely and has spent every night over the last week with me. Why front? He brought me here, and we can't get enough of each other. I'm glad we're on this yacht with a bunch of couples who *also* can't get enough of each other because we'd be pretty obnoxious otherwise.

He's rich as hell and could shower me with material things. And he does. At every port, I find some keepsake from the local shops he's left for me in the room—an ankle bracelet, clips for my hair, diamond earrings. There has been no shortage of gifts, but the real gift has been his attention. The way he cares. The man bathes me. He wraps my hair up at night. He washes my face. I don't know what this is, but I feel spoiled. Doted on. Adored. At first I was like…is this cringe? Is it weird? But then I recalled all those times when I didn't feel valued in a relationship. All those times a guy disrespected me by looking at other women all night. All those times I didn't feel this almost embarrassing amount of single-minded focus from a man who's determined I'll know how much he enjoys me. How much he likes me. Cherishes me, even. He's constantly pulling me onto his lap. We sneak away from the group anytime the mood strikes us. Last night at dinner, he fed me from his plate.

From his plate.

Who am I right now?

I'm that girl, living out a fantasy on a half-a-billion dollar yacht floating on dreams along the coast of Italy. Forget Black girl magic. This is pure sorcery, and if it's a spell, we're both under it.

"I would love to know what's going on inside that head right now," Lotus says, chuckling and setting aside the sketches we were reviewing for her Carnival-themed summer line.

"What?" I bite into a smile. "Sorry. I lost my train of thought."

"Hmmmmmmm," Lotus hums. "Wild, wild thoughts, judging by the way you and Naz have been acting."

"Oh, my god." I cover my face and peek through my fingers. "Am I that obvious?"

"Is that a serious question?" Lotus leans back in her chair on the deck and tips her face to the sun. "He's down bad."

"So am I." My smile fades. "This feels like paradise, but there's a lot of real world waiting for us when we get home."

Lotus pushes oversized sunglasses atop her head and sets a sobering gaze on my face. "I don't know the full history of your past with Naz, but I saw parts of that awful documentary SportsCo aired that mentioned your brother. They showed clips of that game, and I know that kind of brought Naz attention he hadn't gotten before, at least in basketball."

"Yeah. My brother resents Naz for what happened."

"It was high school. A really long time ago."

"It was, but that's the point where my brother's life started falling apart. In a lot of ways, he's still there."

"But that wasn't Naz's fault."

"It's irrational, but Cliff's been through a lot. Most of it because of his own bad choices, but he's just getting back on his feet and..." I swallow the emotion, the remembered panic of Mama's frantic call when Cliff overdosed. "I don't want to do anything that would derail him."

"And you're afraid your relationship with Naz would?"

"It wasn't supposed to be a relationship. It was supposed to be a fling because I'm attracted to him. I have been since the day we met. I've wondered more than once how things could have been different for us, had they been different for Cliff, but it's all tangled up. You can't separate the two."

"And now?" Lotus asks. "No one seeing the two of you together would think this ends when we leave this yacht."

"I know." I close my eyes and release a troubled sigh. The thought of losing whatever Naz and I are building together, even at this early stage, stirs a pang of loss.

"Hey." Lotus reaches across the table, her eyes compassionate. "You still have a few days. Enjoy. We'll cross that bridge when we come to it."

"We?" I laugh and lift my brows.

"Yeah, we." Lotus winks. "You're Naz's girl. You're one of us now."

Naz's girl.

That sings in my head and lights me up inside. I'm still processing the implications of what that could mean if it becomes true—if I let it be true—when Lotus's business partners, Yari and Billie, walk up on deck.

"Hey, bitches," Lotus says, her smile easy and loving. "I barely recognized you without your guys attached to your hips."

"They have real jobs and couldn't stay the whole time." Yari sighs, flopping into an empty chair at the table. "And look who's talking. You got a whole baby from your man."

Lotus rubs her little stomach, oiled up with sunscreen in her bikini, and beams. "He got me!"

"I really like these," Billie says, her green eyes widening as she studies the sketches on the table. "Is this for the Carnival theme next summer?"

"Yeah," Lotus says. "Takira's giving me the inside scoop. She's from Trinidad and goes back all the time for Carnival."

"That's so cool." Yari scoops her dark, curly hair into a messy bun, her arms even browner now from the sun than when we started our trip. "Can you teach us how to wine?"

"How to what?" Billie asks, peeking at us from beneath the wide-brim hat offering her fair skin shade. She's a classic redhead and has been careful with the sun.

"It's dancing." I laugh. "And I've never tried to teach anyone how to do it. It's just…in me. I grew up watching my mama and aunts, cousins, sister—it's something in our blood, and as soon as the music starts, it catches me."

"I actually think I'm pretty good." Lotus makes a show of brushing her shoulders off. "If I do say so myself."

"I'd like to see that big belly wining," Yari teases.

"Sun's out." Lotus scrapes her chair back, stands, and smacks her ass. "Buns out. You got anything we can wine to?"

"Anything we can…" I giggle. "Oh, my god, Lo."

"Music!" Her hands go to her slim hips. From the back, you can't even tell the girl is six months pregnant. "Gimme a beat."

Laughing, I look through the playlist on my phone and pull up some

Soca to dance to. Within ten minutes, the four of us are lined up on deck in our bathing suits in various states of wine.

"It's not twerking," I tell them. "So put that out of your mind. And I don't wanna see no hula hoops."

I bend my knees a little, roll my hips to demonstrate, and immediately feel good. It's like serotonin to my system, the mellifluous motion of my limbs, my torso and hips, and the beat that pounds through my blood.

Lotus actually *is* decent. She jokingly claims she learned from watching Rihanna.

At least, I think she's joking.

Yari says she's Dominican and can dance to any beat under the sun. Also, decent.

That Billie, though.

If there's a stage that is pre-beginner, that's Billie.

But she's trying, and we're laughing, the spray from the sea kissing our faces and the sun warming our bare skin.

"Now you pelting waist, gyal," I shout over the music, nearly losing the flow because I'm laughing so hard at Billie *trying*.

My hips are still swimming in the balmy air, the delicate body chain draped over my neck and around my stomach glinting in the sun, when two large hands bracket my waist from behind. I look up to see Naz towering over me, an indulgent smile shaping his lips.

"You gonna teach me?"

The thought of this huge man—six feet, seven inches of athletic grace, but dancing awkwardness—bubbles laughter out of me.

"Them hips weren't made for wining," I tell him, turning into his hug and tipping up to kiss his chin. "How was volleyball?"

"Intense. You'd think the ballers would be the most competitive, but Jared's a savage."

"I can actually see that, but then, you hear him FaceTiming with Angela every night, reading to her in Spanish…major heart melt."

"True. One of his clients, a soccer player, owns a villa in Positano. We'll stay there for a couple of days when we dock for Kenan's birthday party."

At the mention of Kenan's party, my smile dims. After the party, we fly home, and I'll continue with Naz and hide it…or continue and tell Cliff…or not continue at all. Each of those options holds a promise of some heartache.

"You okay?" Naz frowns and searches my face, my eyes.

I don't want the cloud that's hanging over me hanging over *us*, over the time we have left, so I set the worry aside.

"Yeah." I slip my hands around his waist and smile up at him. "I'm fine."

"Did I miss the lesson?" Banner asks, sidling up beside us. "The wine sesh?"

"You did." I laugh. "But I can give you a private lesson later."

"Awesome," she says, her eyes alight with excitement. "Maybe at the villa. We'll be docking soon, so pack a bag!"

Chapter Sixteen

Naz

"Ready?" I ask, nodding to Takira's overnight bag on the floor. "That's all you got?"

"It's only two nights." She lifts the Louis Vuitton weekender. "I've learned to be pretty streamlined when I travel, even if it's just ashore."

"Let me get it," I say, taking the bag from her. A buzzing sound makes me frown. "What's that?"

"What's what, babe?" she asks, walking to the bathroom. "I was about to leave my makeup bag. Now that would be tragic. I promised to do Billie's makeup for the party."

Not only is the sound a buzz, now I feel something vibrating.

"It's like a buzzing sound. I think it's coming from the bag." I set it on the bed. "I can check."

"Oh, shit!" Takira rushes from the bathroom to stand between me and the bed. "Um, I'll get it. It's just… I'll get it."

She doesn't move but licks her lips and shifts her eyes to the floor.

"Well, get it," I say, grinning, because obviously something's up. "What is it? Why don't you want me to see?"

She holds my gaze for a few seconds and then rolls her eyes, releasing a huffing breath. "I did ride your face last night, so I think at this point, no need to front."

"Agreed." I wrap an arm around her waist and pull her into me, dipping to kiss along her jaw. "But I may need you to ride my face again right quick to make sure."

Her eyes drift closed, and she leans into me before popping her eyes back open. "No! We'll be late."

"I said right quick." I laugh, reluctantly releasing her. "Now show me what's buzzing in the bag you're trying to hide from me."

"It's my…" She turns to unzip the bag and digs around to the bottom. "It's this."

She holds up a black device that looks like a…

"Is that a vibrator?" I ask

"Yeah, it's my lucky vibrator," she says, like that's a real thing. "My sister gave it to me for Christmas kind of as a gag gift."

She turns it off and takes it over to her bedside table, dropping it into the open drawer. "I didn't realize it was still in this bag from my last trip. I guess it got…pressed."

I walk over and open the drawer again, looking at the vibrator. "You like it?"

"It's fine. It's not my best one." She fans her face. "My best one? You'd think that thing had the engine of a Mack truck. And my massage gun? That's on the *kids, don't try this at home* level. I come so…" She stops, bites her lip and glances up at me. "Sorry."

"You were saying you come so…"

"I come so hard with that one." She laughs. "This is a weird conversation."

"Tell me more about this menagerie of vibrators you have." I sit on the bed and pull her down beside me. "I think anything that makes you come hard is something I should know about."

"You're serious?" she asks, assessing me with narrowed eyes.

"Yeah. Tell me."

Her gaze goes from disbelieving to speculative to defiant.

"Okay. I love vibrators. They don't cheat on you. They don't insult you when you gain five pounds or complain when your period is on. They don't gaslight you. You come every time and never have to fake it." She holds up one finger and inclines her head. "And…they don't snore."

"I hope I don't do those things either. I mean, I *do* snore a little."

She looks at me knowingly, lips twisted and arms crossed.

"Okay, I snore a lot." I lean into her, pushing her softness down on the bed and bracketing my arms on either side of her face. "But don't ever fake it with me."

"Oh, don't worry." A husky laugh slips past her lips, and she reaches up to trace my eyebrows with one finger. "I haven't had to."

"I don't just mean sex, Kira. No faking between us on anything."

"I thought this was supposed to *be* just sex." A faint smile curls the edges of her mouth as she looks down, away from my eyes trained on her.

"After these two weeks, we could walk away."

"I never said that." I tip up her chin, and a feeling of rightness warms me inside as soon as our eyes meet again. "It's too late for that."

She draws a shaky breath, closes her eyes, and nods. "I know."

Cliff and his troubles hover at the edge of this paradise. I'm not afraid of confronting it all when we get back to the States, but I know it's not as easy for Takira. I'm giving her space to make peace with the fact that it will have to be done. Because me not with her—that's no longer an option. Cupping her face, I drop a kiss on her forehead and push away.

"We gotta go." Standing, I grab her bag and nod to the drawer where she banished the vibrator. "Why don't you bring it?"

"Seriously?" She lifts her brows and looks from me to the drawer. "Some guys aren't down for that."

Grabbing her bag, I walk to the door and open it to the hallway. "Anything that makes you come that hard is coming with us."

Chapter Seventeen
Takira

"That was delicious." I pat my full belly and reach for my third Bellini. "I could get used to this."

"I *am* used to this now," Yari says, swirling the last of her angel hair pasta around a fork. "I need a raise, Lo, so I can afford an Italian chef."

"Done!" Lotus toasts with her wine glass filled with water. "If this new line sells like I hope it does, we'll all get raises."

"It'll be fantastic, like everything you do," Kenan says. He frowns at her plate with its remnants of pasta and bread. "You barely ate. You feeling okay?"

"This was my second plate." Lotus cups his face in one small hand. "I'm fine. The baby's fine. We're in a gorgeous Italian villa."

The villa, nestled into the Amalfi Coast, overlooks the Tyrrhenian Sea, has nine bedrooms, two private terraces, a swimming pool with outdoor showers, ancient fireplaces, antiques intermixed with the most modern accoutrements, and a gourmet kitchen our temporary Italian chef made impeccable use of.

"Yeah, nice hook-up, Jared," August says. "This place is fantastic."

"He's been offering it to us for..." He looks to Banner. "How long?"

"Like two years, but we aren't exactly the best about taking vacations," she says wryly. "If I'd known how beautiful it was, we would have come sooner."

"We'll come back." Jared leans over to kiss her hair. "And next time, we'll bring the girls."

She serves a grin to everyone at the table. "Jared's convinced we'll have all girls."

"All?" Yari asks, brows lifted. "How many kids y'all trying to have?"

"Three," Jared says.

"Four," Banner says at the same time, laughing and leaning her head on her husband's shoulder. "We're negotiating."

"I think we're done," Iris says. "I thought I wanted more, but I'm hitting a stride in my career. Getting my own accounts and making an impact. Firing on all cylinders. Sarai and David feel like enough."

"What do you think, August?" Yari asks, grinning.

August holds his hands up and laughs. "I don't have a uterus. I don't produce milk. My job has me on the road away from my wife and kids half the year, so I say...yes, dear. Whatever you want, dear. I'm satisfied." He kisses Iris's hand. "But I'd be satisfied if all I had was you, baby."

"Okay, number thirty-three," Iris says, rolling her eyes, even as they brim with affection. "You're getting some tonight. No need to lay it on that thick."

August winks. "Insurance."

We all laugh and push away from the table, agreeing to take advantage of the villa's amenities.

"Swim?" Jade asks Kenya.

"Oh, yeah." Kenya stretches. "I been slacking on my regimen. I need to get some laps in."

Jade takes her hand and leads her much taller wife to the stairs. "Let's get our suits."

"Or we could swim without them," Kenya teases.

"Not if I'm out there." Yari laughs. "I don't need to see all that."

"There's a theater in the basement," Banner says, yawning. "We were gonna go watch a movie."

"I have a feeling that movie will be watching you, Ban." Jared pulls her into his side. "You're tired."

"Making a baby has that effect on me." She widens her eyes meaningfully. "Something I didn't have to hide this trip thanks to your big mouth."

"Movies, you said?" He opens the door leading to the basement, lips pressed against a grin.

Iris, August, Lotus, and Kenan decide to play spades out on the terrace.

"We set them twice last time," Iris tells me, rubbing her hands together. "It stings their pride that these two girls whoop their asses. Wanna come watch?"

"I think we'll take a walk," Naz interrupts, looping an arm around my waist. "There's olive and lemon trees in the grove. If you want, Kira?"

I glance up, mesmerized by the look in his eyes. It's not just passion or desire, but adoration. I don't know how it's possible for that look to be real in less than two weeks, but I trust it. I feel it, too.

"A walk sounds good," I say, my breath shallow.

"Okay." Kenan gives us a knowing look. "Enjoy your walk." He puts walk in air quotes, making us laugh, but neither of us deny that we could get up to something out there.

We set off for the garden, walking in silence for a few minutes with our fingers entwined, the only sounds splashes and squeals from the pool, shouts and good-natured bickering from the card game on the terrace, and the click of our footsteps on flagstones leading us deeper into a copse of trees. The scent of lemons wafts thick in the air, their yellow skins gleaming on sturdy branches in the moonlight. The water shimmers in the distance, moonbeams shading it midnight instead of the bright sapphire blue of day. Embedded into the cliff, the lights of Positano's shops and restaurants sparkle like crown jewels overlooking a sea of glass.

"It's breathtaking." I stop to absorb one of the most captivating views of our trip. Of my life. "It's hard to believe it's real and I'm here."

"We are definitely here." Naz takes my hand, leading me deeper into the grove to a wooden bench situated between two olive trees. "Let's sit."

When I kick off my sandals, Naz scoots to the end so I can rest my head in his lap and swing my legs over the bench arm.

"This feels very *Notting Hill*." I tip my head back to catch the faintest of night breezes. "You know that closing scene?"

"The one where Julia Roberts is pregnant?"

"Not that part. Not for a long time." I shake my head. "I got too much to do."

He lifts one of the long braids left loose from my chest, toying with the end. "What do you want? In the future, I mean?"

"To have an A-list clientele. So few of the Black stylists and makeup artists in Hollywood work consistently with A-list clients. My work deserves to be seen on any red carpet and at every premiere."

"I love your confidence," he says softly, bending to kiss my temple. "What about your personal life? Obviously you said no kids yet."

"Not yet, but I do want them. My parents have been married over forty years. They had trouble getting pregnant at first, and Janice came a few years into their marriage."

I giggle, tipping my head back to catch his eyes. "Mama said once her womb got the hang of it, she couldn't stop." I sober. "She lost two between

Janice and Cliff, but then she got pregnant with me almost as soon as Cliff was born."

"And you two have always been close." He says it as fact, not question.

I nod, a touch of sadness invading the garden, disturbing my peace. Soon I may have to hurt one of the men in my life who mean so much to me.

"Is there a place for me?" Naz asks, the timbre of his voice deepening, caressing. "In your future?"

I sit up and turn to face him, tucking one leg beneath me. "Do you want one?"

He gives me a wry look. "I made a fool of myself to get you on this trip, Kira. What do you think?"

"You didn't make a fool of yourself. You just acted out of character. I'm glad you did. It's been the best trip of my life, and I've made new friends."

I cup his jaw, rubbing the shadow of bristles coating the strong line. "I've had you, Naz, and I've never felt more, never wanted anyone the way I want you."

"And next week?" He grasps my wrist, trapping my hand against his face. "When we get back to LA, do you honestly expect me to let you go?"

I swallow, glancing down at the aged wood of the bench between us. "No. I just...I have to figure out what we say to Cliff. The best time to tell him."

"I got an email tonight."

I frown and shoot him a *huh?* look.

"Okay," I say. "And?"

"It was from Myron."

"Myron from St. Cat's?" I ask, stiffening. "What'd he want?"

"Coach Lipton is retiring, and they're asking all of us from his one championship team to come for the ceremony."

I close my eyes and turn to press my back against the bench, letting both feet hit the ground with a thud. "Cliff is just getting over that damn documentary, and now they want to memorialize the night that ruined his life."

"No, now they want to honor a man who devoted *his* entire life to teaching young men a sport he loves. They want some of the men whose lives he impacted to come celebrate a stellar career as one of Texas's winningest high school coaches in history."

"I know. It's an amazing achievement."

"If Coach Lipton hadn't recruited me to St. Cat's senior year, my life wouldn't be what it is now."

"I know."

"Do you? Because it seems like you think other people's lives should revolve around Cliff's, including your own."

"That's not fair."

"I want to be with you."

I suck in a shuddering breath, stand, and put a few feet between me and him on the bench, but I'm unable to look away from the intent in his dark eyes. "Also not fair."

"Why? Because you'll have to do something about this? When this trip is over, *we're* not over, and I'm not pretending we are for Cliff."

"Naz."

"No, listen to me." He stands and reaches me in one long step, tugging me to him by my wrist. "This, what's happened to us, it's fast. I know that. As cautious as I am, do you think I don't know that? But is it two weeks? Or is it twelve years in the making?"

I swallow and don't try to pull away but press into his chest, breathing in his clean, masculine scent.

His hands, big and gentle, drift around to cradle my back. "I've watched you for years."

At his quiet words, I look up. His eyes are set on me, his sensual lips parted on a laugh at himself.

"I saw you announce on social media when you were leaving Houston, moving to the A."

"You did?"

"And then leaving Atlanta, moving to New York." He grins down at me, tracing the shell of my ear and sending shivers down my spine. "When you posted you were leaving New York and coming to LA for *Dessi Blue,* somewhere in my heart, even subconsciously, I said to myself...now I have her. This close, I'll have her, but I didn't know how. All my life, opportunities have found me. Have fallen into my lap."

He hugs me tight and, arms folded under my butt, lifts me off my feet so our faces are level.

"Naz!" I squeal, legs dangling.

"And what happened?" He sets his eyes on mine, humor sifting out of his expression, leaving an intensity that winnows steam through my blood. "You literally fell into my arms at that fashion show. I didn't know how it would happen for us...but I think I knew it would."

I wrap my legs around his waist and link my arms behind his neck, leaning in to capture his lips between mine. He opens instantly, and that's how it's always been with us. Him, a man notoriously private and reserved and content with himself, opened up for me, craving me. He breaks the kiss, and I draw in his breath and the scent of lemons as he presses our foreheads together.

"I'm going to that retirement ceremony," he says, waiting for me to catch his eyes in the moonlight. "I assume Cliff will be there, too. And this thing with him will be resolved."

Chapter Eighteen

Naz

"What are you wearing to the party?" I ask Takira when she steps out of our en suite bathroom in the villa.

It's the night of Kenan's birthday. They've rented out a beach club, and his friends from all over the world have been invited. The group will still be relatively modest in size, but definitely more than the small party that's been sailing with us. It will be a star-studded event.

Takira and I spent a leisurely last day here at the villa—swimming, eating light salads and rich desserts, drinking the limoncello made from the lemons in the grove, and making love with the laughter of our friends floating in on a Mediterranean breeze through our open terrace door.

Takira's fluffy white robe gapes open as she walks into the bedroom after finishing her makeup. Vibrant color splashes across her eyes, cheeks, and lips, complementing the regal upsweep of her braids. The necklace with the diamond T charm she wore to the after-party hangs around her sleek throat, and the set of square diamond earrings I found in Capri adorn her ears.

I open the robe more, touching the elegant line of her shoulders and collarbone, the ripe fullness of her breasts, kissing the smaller right and the slightly bigger left. She giggles, running her hand over my freshly cut hair. Hair she cut out on the terrace this morning when we woke. I slip my finger between the firm, rounded cheeks of her ass.

"I'm gonna fuck you here." When I caress the puckered entrance, a shudder racks her curvy body. "One day soon."

"I was hoping you'd say that."

"Oh, you were?" I go down on my knees, pull her leg over my

shoulder, and kiss her pussy with my open mouth, sucking her clit. Biting.

"Naz." She grips my other shoulder. "Do that shit again."

I chuckle against the soft lips, kissing her there, licking into her. "You're so pretty right here. And I love the way you taste. I'm the only one who gets to see and taste you anymore, right?"

I look up, checking her face for compliance or any sign that she doesn't agree. I don't have vows or a ring or even a damn declared relationship. She's still deciding if she'll choose me over the loyalty she has to her brother, but the thought of her with someone else sends a ripple of rage through every fiber of my being. I've never been possessive, but this woman was made for me, and if I get my way, from now on, she'll only be mine and I'll only be hers. I wonder if it was supposed to be that way all along, and the thing that took me to fame, to fortune, also took me away from the woman who could have made me happy all these years.

"Just you," she whispers, affirms. "Unless you get the urge to watch some girl eat me out."

I pause, the image stirring something low in my chest that moves down to my dick. My eyes flash up to meet hers, filled with wicked enjoyment. She bends until her lips brush my ear.

"I *know* you, Naz." She bites my earlobe. "Whenever you want it, baby."

I'm hard and ready at the image, at her offer. She lowers her leg from my shoulder and walks to the closet, grinning, all mischief. "Just something to think about."

Minx. My minx.

She pulls out a dress of unrelieved white, lays it on the bed, and steps into her thong, the rounded cheeks of her ass exposed in the tiny underwear.

"What are you wearing?" She lobs my question back to me. "Everyone has to wear white, remember."

"I've got something," I say, my voice still rough. "But let me dress you."

"Go right ahead."

She holds her arms out to the side, standing before me nearly naked, long legs stretching forever and breasts ripe and proud. Her skin gleams a deeper brown from all the sun of the last two weeks, beautiful and burnished.

I'm unable to take my eyes off her. I push her gently to the bed, grab the body cream she always uses from the bedside table, and scoop a generous amount into my hands. I work it into her heels and the arches of her feet, smiling when her toes twitch. I smooth it over the satiny skin of her calves and knees and thighs. I use a little more for her arms, back, and shoulders, tangling our gazes when I take time to work it into the soft mounds of her breasts. Her breath hitches and her stomach muscles contract as I rub it into her nipples. I pull her to her feet and slip the dress over her head. It clings to her shape, the cut-outs leaving her sides completely bare, from her hips to just below her breasts.

She inspects herself in the mirror for a second, turning to check the cut-outs. "We got some side boob."

"I noticed," I say approvingly. "I'll be lucky to make it through the night without ripping this dress off you."

"Don't try too hard," she says with a wink.

Turning her back to the mirror, she peers over her shoulder. "I can barely wear this thong with it. Maybe I should go without."

"If you take off those panties, trust and believe you're getting fucked in a public place tonight."

"Promise?" Her dark eyes dance with humor, and something squeezes around my heart. She's so bold and smart and kind and hilarious. She makes me laugh and lust and live life to the fullest. Usually reticent, I find that I want to tell her *everything*. I'm not sure she's ready to hear how deeply the last two weeks have affected me.

"Sit." I nod to the bed. Once she's seated, I grab the shoes she's set out and slip them on her feet, glancing up to meet her eyes.

I tug her to stand and walk her over to the wall mirror, standing behind her and entwining our fingers at her sides. With her braids coiled into an intricate updo, studded with gold clamps, and the proud set of her shoulders as she stares back at her reflection, she looks like a queen.

"You really enjoy doing this for me, don't you?" she asks, something like wonder in her eyes.

"You're obviously incredibly capable," I tell her. "I know you don't *need* me to take care of you, but I want you to know there's someone who loves doing it. That you don't have to carry everything alone."

She looks stunned for a moment. I bend to kiss her cheek and then the corner of her mouth.

"For someone who works so hard making other people beautiful," I tell her, "for a few days, I wanted you not to lift a finger even for yourself."

"No one's ever done that for me." She blinks rapidly, biting her bottom lip.

I turn her back to study her reflection and meet her eyes in the mirror. "I hope you'll get used to it."

Chapter Nineteen

Takira

The beach club isn't that large, but it's spectacular. Decorated entirely in white and gold, it's somehow pristine and decadent. The supple leather couches and seats, the crystal chandeliers sparkling with diamond brilliance overhead, the mirrored bars—all of it should scream excess but somehow merely whispers opulence. The dance floor juts out onto the water, creating the illusion that it's floating. Boats of various sizes are moored at the edges like a watery parking lot. Our yacht is a little farther out but looms as a grim reminder that it and the end of this idyllic trip are waiting for me.

"Having fun?" Iris asks over the music. She looks beautiful, her dark hair piled atop her head and a slinky dress molded to her curves. Nothing about her says "mother of two," but I've seen her texting and talking on the phone with August's mom, who has their kids—seen her FaceTiming with them. She's a devoted mom. A hot one, too.

"The party's great," I reply. "That dress is gorgeous, by the way."

"Yours!" Her eyes sweep over me. "You look so good, but you always do. So confident."

"Confident or don't care what nobody thinks. I'm a little of both, I guess."

"You're exactly what Naz needs. He's kind of reserved, and a bold woman like you to shake things up is good for him."

"He's good for me, too."

"Well, I'm glad he tricked you into coming," Iris says, her lips quirking.

"It wasn't much of a trick," I say wryly. "My eyes were pretty wide open."

I survey the party, packed with people I've seen on E! and TMZ and occasionally around town back in LA.

"Kenan has a lot of friends," I tell Iris with a smile.

"He's a good guy to have in your corner, so everyone wants him in theirs. He's pretty discriminating about who he lets in, though, so if they're here, they're good people."

"Where are the guys?" I ask, realizing I haven't seen any of them for a while.

"Believe it or not, there's a wall-sized television on the other side of the club. They're all watching some soccer match. Jared's client's playing." She grabs a drink from a tray as it passes. "But I'm going to retrieve my husband right now."

"I need to find Naz, too." I search the floor of gyrating bodies and check the room's perimeter lined with couches where partygoers are eating, drinking, lounging. No sign of Naz.

"Oh, isn't that him?" Iris points across the room to a far corner.

My eyes find him easily, his height and shoulders making him a mountain in a roomful of trees. He, like everyone else, wears white, and the open collar shirt paired with tailored white slacks shows stark against his dark skin. His proud head is tilted down to a blonde woman, a server holding a tray and speaking into his ear.

"Yup," I say, a small smile on my lips. "You go find your man while I go get mine."

Iris smirks sweetly. "Go easy on her."

"No, ma'am."

He sees me first, meeting my eyes over her shoulder and smiling that slow smile that says *I woke up this morning with my dick in your mouth.*

"Hello," I say, pulling up beside him and staring pointedly at the beautiful platinum blonde with the dark eyes. "Naz, honey, introduce me to your friend."

"Of course." He slips an arm around my waist and drops a kiss on top of my head. "This is Giovanna. She works here. Giovanna, this is my girl, Takira."

Giovanna's smile freezes and then shrivels, her panicked eyes flitting between Naz and me.

"Oh, I…" Her Italian accent is thick, and her Italian features are striking. "It's nice to meet you. I was just saying…I was asking—"

"Apparently there's a room in the back where couples sometimes…" Naz waggles his brows. "You know."

"Oh." I clap my hands under my chin. "I wanna see."

There's a dense silence following my words. Giovanna's expression goes from awkward to interested in half a second flat.

"*Sì.*" She nods enthusiastically and grabs my hand, heading for a corridor at the rear of the club.

"Kira." Naz grabs my other hand, pulling us all to a halt. "We don't need to—"

"Come on," I coax.

Our eyes hold for a few seconds before he concedes and inclines his head for Giovanna to lead us. We weave our way down the long passageway lined with doors. Giovanna holds one of my hands, and Naz holds the other. When we reach the last door, he tugs me to his side and eyes Giovanna, his expression impassive.

The door swings open to reveal a room with a plush couch against the wall and the same marble floor that runs the length of the hallway.

"See?" Giovanna sings, eyeing us both, her smile growing wider when she closes and locks the door. "Private."

She takes a step toward Naz and presses her hand to his chest, and I clasp her wrist, carefully lifting her hand away.

"That's as far as you go," I say. "I'll take it from here."

Giovanna freezes, confusion on her pretty face and in her luminous, dark eyes. She pouts and looks between the two of us like we stole her toys before she leaves. In the quiet that follows, I step up to Naz, subtly inching him back until we reach the couch. I push his shoulder, and he sits, looking up at me with ravenous eyes. I bend to place my knees on either side of his spread thighs, straddling him, my dress fanning out over his lap in a flurry of silk.

He strokes the exposed skin of my back. "I don't want anyone but you."

"And I don't want anyone but you." I dip my head, taking his mouth in a kiss so carnal, it burns my lips and sets fire to my blood. With tomorrow taunting me, closing in on our Utopia, I clutch his strong arms, clasp his face between trembling hands, rock my hips over his erection. The friction through the thin lace of my thong arrows desire in me and steals the breath from my lungs and every thought but him from my mind. His hand slips into the side cut-out of my dress to palm my breast beneath the silk, pinching my nipple.

"You want to choke me, I'm down," I breathe in his ear. "You want to fuck me in the ass, you can. You want Giovanna to come back and eat me out while you watch, you can have that, too. I love making you feel good. Just tell me what you want."

I seal the offer with a kiss that gives him everything I promised and more. It lifts every barrier between us. Even still clothed, my words and the greedy, compulsive need winding between us strip us naked. I'm putty in his hands, and he's putty in mine, and with every touch, we mold each other into exactly what the other needs, while never losing ourselves.

"Tell me you're mine," he whispers into our kiss, his voice raw, his hands desperate, clenching on my thighs, urging the flowing skirt higher to expose my thong.

"I just did." I laugh against his lips.

"I'm serious, Kira." He leans his head away when I move to kiss him again. "We fly back tomorrow."

"I know." I take the collar of his shirt between my fingers and raise my eyes no higher than his Adam's apple. "You'll go back to San Diego?"

"In the off-season, I live in LA. Not far from Kenan and Lotus." He cups my face and presses his forehead to mine. "Come stay with me."

A startled gasp slips past my lips. "It's only been two weeks."

"I'm not saying move in, but just keep doing what we've been doing." He trails kisses down my throat and peels the dress back, kneading my breast. "Eating together, sleeping together, learning each other."

I can barely focus on his words with his hand at my breast and his eyes so intent on my face. Suspecting that's what he's counting on, I force myself to pull back until his hand drops away.

"I know this whole trip put the cart before the horse," I say, pulling my dress and my sanity back into place. "But I'd rather take our time."

"You want to stop sleeping together?" he asks, his expression unchanging. "We can do that."

"Oh, hell no." I reach between us to palm him through his pants. "Give this up when I just learned to ride it?"

He smiles and caresses the cleft in my chin, his eyes softening. "Then tell me what you want."

I shrug, feeling self-conscious for some reason. Maybe because it exposes the girl who through the years stopped believing in fairy tales but now finds herself in the arms of a prince.

"I want us to make plans and to feel anticipation as I get dressed, knowing the doorbell will ring and it's you. I want to kiss you goodnight and get the chance to miss you when you're gone. I want to wonder when I'll see you again." I run a hand over the back of my neck. "It's silly, I—"

"I'd like that, too." He kisses my nose, smiling. "I want to spoil you."

I tip back on his lap and laugh. "I hope you don't expect me to stop you."

A knock on the door interrupts whatever we would have said next. It creaks open to show Yari with her hand over her eyes.

"I'm not looking." She peers through the crack of her fingers. "I mean, maybe a little."

I swing my legs over and off Naz's lap and straighten out my dress. "Nothing to see here."

"If you say so." She turns back toward the door. "I came to find you because they're about to cut the cake."

"Oh, yay." I move to follow her, but Naz pulls me up short.

"Hey, about what you asked for," he says, his smile as dazzling as the chandeliers out front. "I'm going to court you like you deserve."

"You old school." I laugh. "And old-fashioned."

"You like it." He pulls me toward the door. I dig my heels in, stopping so that he turns a querying look to me. I look straight into his eyes. No teasing. No humor. No confusion or even guilt.

"I like *you*," I say, squeezing his hand for emphasis.

"I know," he says, stepping out into the hall and leading me toward the music drifting from the dance floor. "I mean, I got to third base with you the night we met, so I figured."

"Oh, my god!" My cheeks go hot, despite the fact that we've done much freakier things since that night on the roof senior year. "Mama would have plucked me like a chicken if she'd caught us."

"Cliff caught us instead."

I'm silent, letting the prickly situation with Cliff still ahead nick my happy bubble for a second.

"It'll be fine. I'll do whatever I have to do to make it work with Cliff." He lifts my chin and searches my eyes. "You trust me?"

The confidence and earnestness in his eyes settle the unease gripping my heart, even if only for the next few minutes. How could I not trust him? I nod and lean into him for our last few steps into the main room. We melt into the crowd that's waiting and watching the stage. He pulls me close, my back to his front and his arms linked over my middle.

"Good evening, everyone,'" Lotus says from the stage positioned in the middle of the room. She wears a white floor-length cape dress that bares one shoulder. "Thank you for traveling to celebrate Kenan's birthday with us."

Kenan stands beside her, watching her with so much adoration, I feel like a voyeur. Like an interloper observing something so intimate between them, even though it's just a glance. I wonder how long it will take for me to look at Naz that way.

Unless I already do?

Two servers wheel a huge, multi-tiered white cake onto the stage.

"Before we cut this masterpiece of a cake," Lotus says, "I want to make a toast to my husband, my best friend, my soul mate."

Lotus closes her eyes briefly, pressing her lips tight as if fighting for control of her emotions.

"Kenan," she says. "You're the pushiest patient man I've ever met."

A light ripple of amusement flows through the crowd.

"You were determined to get your shot with me," Lotus says, "and you did."

Kenan only nods, his expression sober, his attention completely on Lotus, who grips her hands in front of her waist, the richness of her sun-browned skin a startling contrast to the snowfall of her dress. I'm not sure if they even need any of us in this moment, they're so intent on each other.

"When we met," Lotus continues, "I wasn't looking. I was deliberately *not* looking, actually, and had sworn off dating altogether."

She holds his stare while servers distribute glasses of champagne to the crowd.

"But to quote one of my favorite pieces, the Song of Songs, 'I have found the one whom my soul loves.' I always tease you about the difference in our ages, but I want you to know I relish every year we've had so far and covet every year ahead."

He cups her face with one huge hand and kisses her forehead, leaning to whisper in her ear. Whatever he says, he doesn't care that we can't hear. It elicits a trembling smile from his beautiful wife.

"Sorry, y'all," she laughs, turning tear-bright eyes back to the crowd. "That was just for me."

"I told her that when I get her home," Kenan says with a shameless grin, "I'mma—"

Lotus goes up on her toes to reach him, slamming her hand over his wide smile.

"Like I was saying," she laughs, holding up a champagne glass undoubtedly filled with something non-alcoholic. "Happy birthday to the finest man I know."

"Happy birthday!" we shout, sipping our champagne and oohing when balloons fall from the ceiling and confetti explodes from every direction. Amid the celebratory chaos, a sobering thread of realization runs through me like a fraying ribbon. Seeing Kenan and Lotus on stage, witnessing their devotion to each other, gives me a picture of what I could have—what I thought I maybe never would after all the app date disasters and failed attempts at relationships. Kenan and Lotus, Banner and Jared, August and

Iris—all the couples we sailed with for the last few weeks have extraordinary marriages. Within a few minutes of being around them, you recognize a rare bond that most people never find.

But what if I've found it?

Naz and I have only been together two weeks, and it's amazing. Beyond anything I've ever had. And it's not just the outstanding, once-in-a-lifetime sex—though that's worth mentioning. It's how I feel when I'm with him. Who I am with him and who he is with me.

I have found the one whom my soul loves.

Lotus quoted that in her toast. What if I have found the one? Or he found me? Or I fell into his arms? Whatever. Fate, the universe—something threw us together again, and I have to believe it's for a reason.

With Cliff's judgment and his fragile recovery at stake, the question becomes *Is the possibility of what this thing between Naz and me could be...worth it?*

Kenan bends to kiss Lotus's baby bump, and the blatant love on his face when he looks down at her, when she returns the look a hundredfold...I can't help but think it is.

Chapter Twenty

Takira

"I'm on my way." Naz's deep voice on speaker sends a frisson of pleasure over me.

"Good," I reply, looking in the mirror at my half-done makeup. "I'll be ready."

"I haven't been to many premieres and I haven't seen much of Canon's work, to be honest."

"Well, this is a documentary." My hands dither between the Pat McGrath and Tarte eye shadow palettes. "So not quite as glamorous as the *Dessi Blue* premiere will be, but everything Canon makes garners attention."

"I can't wait to show you off on the red carpet," he says, the same pride in his voice that's always there when we go out.

"Um, about that…" I sit in front of the mirror, dreading this conversation. "I was thinking maybe we shouldn't walk the red carpet tonight."

The silence on the other end of the phone clogs up with his frustration before he agrees and we hang up. He already knows why. In the two weeks since we've been back, we've seen each other every day, every night. Sometimes he stays at my place. Sometimes I'll stay over at his. Sometimes…we say good night at the door and I ache for him, but it's a sweet ache because I know I'll see him again. Sweet because I know he's aching, too. It's a *relationship*. Not a one-night stand, a hook-up, a booty call, a fling, or a smash and grab.

It's us, and it feels as fragile as a bubble blown and floating in the air— as strong as an oak tree that has withstood storms. It's playing catch-up and it's ahead of its time.

It's everything I had become too jaded to believe in or hope for.

Only one spot has marred such a perfect start.

I still haven't told Cliff. Or my parents, for that matter. Of course, Janice knows, and keeps urging me to tell them. She says *rip the Band-Aid off.* It's a point of contention between Naz and me, so we don't talk about it much. He's not going anywhere, and I don't want him to. But at some point, I'll have to tell Cliff. He's just doing so well with his job, with his kids, with his life. Better than he's been in a long time. If I did anything to hurt that, I'd never forgive myself. I'm not giving up Naz, though. My love for my brother and my...*feelings* for Naz are on a collision course.

It's too soon to say *love.*

Right?

I don't know that I've ever actually been in love before, but if it feels any deeper, any richer than this—if it moves you more—I may not be able to stand it.

I check the mirror propped against the wall in my bedroom.

Damn, I look good.

It's not just the silk dress that clings to all my curves from breast to thigh and then ends with a flare of tulle above my knees. Or the perilously high heels that tie up in straps around my calves. With my braids gone, I've styled my natural hair into a frothy halo of textured waves and curls. To garnish the sexy image, my diamond T charm glints against the lingering tan of my throat. I'm putting the finishing touches on my lipstick when the phone rings again. I grab it and glance at the screen.

Mama.

My heart seizes a little every time I see her name onscreen. I know it's ridiculous, but I flash back to the night she called screaming and crying so much I couldn't understand a word she said. And once I did understand, the horror of what had happened to Cliff... I'll never forget that. I shake off the memory and answer.

"Hey, Mama."

"Tee, hey, baby. How you?"

Some of the leftover tension drains from my shoulders as her accent breezes over me, stronger today, as it often is after she talks with any of our family still living in Trinidad.

"I'm good. How you?"

"Fine. You talk to Neecey?"

"We texted yesterday." I sit on the edge of my bed and admire how the white polish on my toes looks with my tan. "Everything okay?"

"I just got off the phone with her not too long ago." A brief pause breaks the flow of Mama's words. "You heard about that retirement thing they're doing for Coach Lipton?"

I draw in a deep breath and blow it out before answering. "I heard something about it, yeah."

"They've asked Cliff to say a few words."

"That's good. He loves Coach and Coach loves him—has been there for him through everything."

"True. I just worry. He's been doing so good, and I don't want no setbacks, ya know?"

"Of course. He'll be fine, don't you think?"

"Praying, but I thought it might be good if you and Janice maybe come home to visit? Support him?"

"Oh." It's all I can manage for a second.

"Janice isn't sure she'll be able to get away. She's checking. If you're busy, I understand, but I heard Nazareth is attending, too, and you know how that boy sets Cliff off."

Hearing Naz's name from her jars me, and for a moment, it's like a glitch—something in the wrong place and time. Images of Naz I've collected over the last month fill my mind. Him leaning against the rail on the yacht, his smile wide and blinding. Laughing, holding my hand as we explored the streets of Positano. His stern features softened in the waning light of the villa's garden surrounded by lemon and olive trees. And all of our dates since we've been back in LA.

Not telling her about Naz feels like a betrayal to all he and I have shared.

"Mama," I say, my voice coming out stronger than I thought it would. "There's something I need to tell you."

"Out wit' it, Tee."

"It's about Naz."

"Nazareth?" The silence on the other ends blooms and ripens. "What about him?"

"He and I…" I blow out a breath. "I ran into him here in LA."

"And?" she asks, the knowing loud in her softly asked question.

"We're seeing each other."

"Ahhhh. How long this been going on?"

"About a month. The trip to Italy—it was with him."

"Takira." Her chuckle on the other end of the line surprises me. "You don't ever make things easy, do you?"

I find myself laughing back, shaking my head. "I guess not. What do you think Cliff will say?"

"He won't like it. You know this, but he's a grown man, right?"

"Do you think seeing Naz at the ceremony or finding out about us will set him back?"

I want her to say no. I want her to tell me it's silly to even think so, but she found him. She was more traumatized by it than any of us.

"I don't know," she finally admits. "That boy…lots wasted, but he's got a lot of life still ahead of him. He'll have to decide what he's gonna do with it. You can't live for him, though. None of us can, and I've been guilty of that more than once."

"I…I care about Naz," I tell her, my resolve strengthening. "And I'm not giving him up."

"All right now," Mama says, sounding pleased. "Even more reason for you to come for the ceremony. That's something Cliff needs to hear from you. *You* need to be the one to tell him."

Her suggestion is still ringing in my ears when Naz arrives at my door a few minutes later.

"Hey," I greet him with a pleased smile.

"Hey." He bends to kiss me briefly, but his demeanor is subdued when he enters the apartment. He looks handsome and austere in his impeccably tailored dark jacket and slacks.

"Are you mad at me?" I ask, my voice sounding more uncertain than I'm used to it being, and I hate that.

He glances up, his full lips tightening, and takes the few strides that bring him back to me at the front door. He leaves me no space, placing his arms on either side of me, pressing his forehead to mine.

"I'm not mad at you, Kira," he says, a raw edge to his voice. "I'm in love with you."

A startled breath chuffs past my lips. I can't pretend the notion hasn't crossed my mind, crossed my heart, but we haven't *said* it. I thought it was too soon, thought we should be more sure, but there is absolute certainty in the eyes that burn into mine, and that look finds an echo inside of me. An answer to his call.

"I love you," he says again. "And I don't want to hide that from the world by not walking a stupid red carpet that I usually don't even care about but want to walk with you."

"Naz—"

"And I for damn sure don't want to hide it from your family." He drops his nose to the juncture of my neck and shoulder. "But I will. If you aren't ready to tell Cliff—if you're scared it will set him back—that matters more to me than my desire to tell the world how I feel."

He scoffs, shaking his head. "Me, who has always guarded my private life wanting to tell the world anything is crazy, but this…" He places a large, warm hand over my heart. "This, I want the world to know."

"We kind of scooted right past the part where you said you love me," I whisper, looking up at him, emotion burning my throat and tears welling in my eyes. "That seems important."

"More important than keeping it from Cliff? From your family and the rest of the world?"

I ease up on my toes and spread my hand over his neck, drawing him down until only a breath separates our lips.

"Considering I love you, too," I say, not heeding the tears slipping over my cheeks, "it seems more important than everything."

He takes my lips or I take his—I don't know which, but we take each other, and there's somehow no end or beginning to it. This didn't start twelve years ago on the rooftop of my house under a quarter moon. It didn't begin under the Mediterranean sun or idling on the sea. It feels like it started when I was born, and everything in my life brought me to him and him to me—like all the times we were apart were held breaths, and here together, in each other's arms, we can finally breathe.

He pulls away, one hand under my dress, gripping my thigh, the other palming my ass.

"Shit." He lowers his head again, kisses me again like it's a compulsion, an involuntary action he can't or won't even try to stop. "If we don't go now, we won't go, and I won't care."

"No." I give him a gentle shove. "We're going. We have a red carpet to walk."

He does a double take, a smile spreading across his face. "Are you sure?"

"Yes. I'll call Cliff tomorrow. I don't know how he'll respond, but we'll deal with it as best we can. Besides." I execute a slow turn, making sure he sees every curve from every angle. "I'm always making sure everyone else is ready for their big moments." I smile, grabbing his fingers with one hand and the doorknob with the other. "It's my turn now, and I'm ready for my close-up."

Chapter Twenty-One
Takira

"What's up, Tee?" my brother asks, sounding like half his attention is on our conversation and half elsewhere.

"You got a sec?"

"Anything for my little sis," he says, still sounding absentminded.

"What did I interrupt?" I find myself smiling in spite of his distractedness.

"I was drawing up some plays."

"It's summer. The season won't start 'til the fall. You've got some time."

"True, but I can't stop thinking about what we might do next year. We got a great group of guys." He sighs. "Anyway, lemme stop. My baby sister is on the line. Big-time stylist to the stars."

There's no mockery in his voice, only pride, and the tightness in my chest eases. He's been through a lot; he's put us through a lot, but when it comes down to it, he's still my big brother who I loved more than just about anything growing up, even when he was a jerk. In spite of it all, he's still my Trini twin.

"I don't want to hold you." I clear my throat. "So I'll get right to it. I'm seeing someone."

"Ahhh," he says, teasing, knowing. "Boy or girl?"

I release a shallow, nervous laugh. "Boy."

"Well, tell me about him. He must be special. You never bother telling me about the jerks you meet on Tinder and shit."

"You, uh, you know him, actually."

"For real? Know him like a celebrity out there in Hollywood, or know him—"

"Personally. You knew him back in the day." Impatience with my own stalling rushes the words out of me. "It's Nazareth, uh…Naz Armstrong."

My words reverberate in the silence that follows them.

"What the fuck, Tee?" he explodes. "You shitting me?"

I flinch. Even braced for his disapproval, I'm still shaken by his anger. "No, I ran into him in LA and—"

"And out of all the guys you could've fucked, it had to be him? The one who took my place? Ruined everything for me? Is that it? Wanted you a baller?" He expels a harsh breath. "My own sister. Chasing clout and giving up ass for—"

"Fuck you, Cliff," I say, my voice low and lethal in a way I reserve for him when he's showing his ass. "I love you, and it's been hard to watch what's happened to you since that game, but you made those choices. It wasn't Naz's fault. None of it. You hit that coach. You started using. Accept responsibility for it."

"You have no idea how it feels to have everyone turn on you." His voice hardens, sounding so brittle I'm afraid it will break. "To have all you did your whole life count for nothing because of one bad call."

I'm not sure if he means that ref's bad call, or his bad decision-making in the wake of it, but I let him go on.

"And you don't know how it burns," he says, the words seething from hundreds of miles away, "to see someone you know is less talented get it all. Get the scholarship that was meant for you. Get drafted instead of you. Win a ring instead of you. It's like he's living my life, Tee."

"I understand but—"

"He got it all," he plows over my protest. "And now you tell me he even got my sister?"

"Our relationship isn't about you, Cliff," I say, trying to keep my tone even, reasonable, even though panic and frustration and anger and fear whir inside me like a typhoon.

"Of course it's not about me. It's about him. My whole life seems to always come back to him. Scrub ass, taking everything meant for me."

"Look, I'm coming home next week. We can talk about it more when I get there."

"Oh, yeah. I heard he was coming to the ceremony. The big baller who made it coming to share a few words with the little people he left behind. What? You his date?"

"No, I'm not coming with him. I'm…I'm coming for you. Mama thought—"

"Mama thought I might start using because I just couldn't take Naz's success? Seeing him again?"

"I'm coming because—"

"I may not be a big-time baller, a millionaire like your new boyfriend, but I have my job and my kids. I ain't jeopardizing that for him."

"Good." Even though this went as badly as I'd thought it would, I take some heart from that reassurance. "I'm glad to hear that. When I come next week, we can—"

"Don't bother."

And the line goes dead.

Chapter Twenty-Two

Naz

It feels strange being here again.

Houston hasn't felt like home in a long time. When I was drafted to Seattle, Mama moved out West to be closer to me. My sisters all married and settled with their families elsewhere. So there's nothing here for me.

Well, there's one thing in this city for me right now.

Takira is at her mother's house. Even though her brother, that motherfucker, went off on her and told her not to attend the ceremony, she made the trip anyway. She opted to stay at her parents' house instead of with me at the hotel, which is probably wise considering the circumstances but still pisses me off. I'm not sure if Cliff even knows she's here. When I talked to her earlier, she hadn't seen him. He hadn't come by the house.

I walk the halls of St. Catherine's, and it's like I've been transported back to that year when I felt so out of place, felt like I didn't fit anywhere, not even with the team I had come to play ball with. The closer I get to the gym where the ceremony is being held, the more I'm ready to get out of here. I'm doing this to honor Coach Lipton and for no other reason. He believed in me when I barely believed in myself. I'll see him, say a few words, and get out.

When I reach the gym, I stare at the glass display case just beyond its doors. The retired jerseys hang in that case. From our senior class, there are only two. Fletcher's because he broke every record any baller ever set in this place. And mine because I'm the only guy from our class who went on to play in the pros.

"Strongarm!"

No one's called me that in years, and I turn toward the name with a frown.

"Myron?"

"Yup." He preens, rubbing the goatee on his chin. "Look the same, huh? Ain't aged a day."

He actually hasn't. Seeing him so unchanged makes me feel even more like I've gone back in time.

"Glad you could make it," he says. "It'll mean a lot to Coach."

"Wouldn't miss it." I nod toward the open door of the gym. "He in there?"

"Yeah. Let's get this party started."

I follow him into the packed auditorium and take a seat on the front row reserved for speakers. The crowd, full of players and parents, faculty and staff—past and present—cheers when Coach Lipton waves at them from the stage. It is a party—a celebration of a stellar career and a legacy of teaching and service. It's the send-off Coach Lipton deserves, and I'm glad I came, even if I do feel Cliff's anger from a few seats away. I don't bother looking at him, selfish asshole. When it's my turn to speak, I keep it simple. If I say too much about my career or the success I've had, even in the context of thanking Coach for his part in it, it might set Cliff off. I'm already having to hold myself back after Takira told me how he treated her during their call. No need to provoke him or myself.

"And now we'll hear from the guy who carried this team while he was here," Myron says, smiling at his old friend. "Our captain, Cliff Fletcher."

The applause is thunderous. I'm not sure if it's for all he accomplished while he was here or supporting him because of how he fell when he left, but I join in. Even if I don't want to, I do for Takira. And because, dammit, though the drugs have aged him and addiction took a heavy toll, denting his good looks, I still can't see him without seeing her.

"We're here to honor a great man," Cliff says at the mic, looking out over the crowd. "Coach Lipton, you taught me a lot. You taught us all a lot."

His laugh is hollow. His grimace comes and goes. "Some of us never learned. You instructed us as much off the court as you did on, Coach. Character, you used to say, always trumps stats."

He pauses, swallowing and glancing down at the floor.

"I had to learn that the hard way, I guess," he says. "It didn't matter how many records I broke or where they hung my jersey, when I was selfish and foolish, reckless, no one cared about my stats. I failed in character. I failed my team. I failed my coach and my family. I failed myself."

It's totally silent as Takira's brother breaks in front of everyone. Not crying or making a scene, but breaking off, piece by prideful piece. Humbling himself. Or is it life that's humbled him?

When I look at him now, it's through Takira's eyes. I see the big brother she adored and would do anything to protect—to shield. I see him warning the team off his sister because she was too good for all of us.

He was right about that.

They shared a special bond, and for me—because by some miracle, she loves me—she put her relationship with him at risk.

I had every intention of making a beeline for the door, going straight to my hotel, calling Takira and trying to convince her to meet me somewhere. Anywhere. But when the ceremony ends, I first have to make my way over to Coach Lipton and thank him personally for all he did for me.

"Armstrong," he says, patting my shoulder. "Thank you for coming. So proud of you, son."

"Thank you"—I step back and look him in his eyes—"for seeing my potential and recruiting me. For giving me a shot. You had a huge impact on me."

"Aww. Just..." He blinks, his throat moving with a deep swallow. "Just doing my job. How's your mother? Your sisters?"

He moves to small talk because I suspect his emotions tonight are hard to keep under control. Having said my piece, I turn to leave, only to come face to face with Cliff.

"Fletcher," I say, barely sparing him a glance, and move to walk around him.

"Wait." His hand snakes out and grabs my arm.

I look from the grip he has on me to his face. Is he really going to do this shit on Coach's big night? I don't answer but stare at him, waiting.

"I need to talk to you," he says, tipping his head toward the gym exit.

Tension rises around us as people watch our interaction. If he's gonna show out, the least we can do is go somewhere everyone won't see it.

"Sure." I shrug and head for the exit without checking to see if he's following.

Once we're in the hall, he glances at the glass case, his mouth assuming a bitter twist.

"I, um, I owe you an apology," he says.

My eyes snap to his face, disbelief freezing me in place and keeping me silent.

"I've talked about you a lot over the years." He scoffs. "To my sponsor, to doctors in rehab, to my family—to anyone who would listen to how you had ruined my life."

I wait, wondering what changed since he talked to Takira last week.

"I had stopped going to group for a while," he says. "After that last time I relapsed, I couldn't face them. Felt like such a failure."

"You went back?" I ask because he's the one doing all the talking, and I don't want him to think I'm not engaged, not really hearing him.

"Last week, yeah." He glances at me, and his eyes are so much like Takira's, but so much older, so much wearier, it makes my chest tighten. I know how much she loves him, and his pain is hers. And now hers is mine.

"When Kira told me about you and her…" He draws a sharp breath through his nose, rubs his mouth. "I was pissed. I kept thinking, him? Of all people, him? The guy who got everything that was supposed to be mine?"

I don't correct him. At times I've felt the same way, even though I know it's not actually true, a kind of survivor's remorse.

"Believe me," he goes on, "Mama has told me a million times I'm wrong. Everyone told me at some point, and I know it's true."

"You do?" I ask, my voice gruff with skepticism.

"It's easier to blame you than to see in you all I could have been and had," he says, a muscle clenching along his jaw. "And know I got nobody to blame but me." He looks me in the eyes. "So I'm sorry. It's overdue by years, but I'm sorry."

"I appreciate that," I tell him, nodding. "In a short time, I've come to care about your sister a lot. Scratch that. I'm in love with her."

His stare is glued to my face.

"I hope one day we'll be related," I say with a wry smile, ignoring the surprise flashing across his expression. "And I want a better relationship with you, so I need to tell you something from jump."

"All right," he says. "Yeah,"

I pause, give it a second to make sure he's looking right into the sobriety of my eyes. "If you ever disrespect Takira again like you did last week," I say quietly, "I'll fuck you up."

"She's my sister," he says, not with anger, but just as a statement of fact.

"If you treat her like it, we won't have a problem."

For a moment, tension coils between us again, and I'm not sure he won't punch me the way he did that coach, but then he cracks a wide smile.

"My man," he says, patting me on the back. "Better you than me. She's a handful to protect."

I release a laugh, surprised and relieved by his comment. "I know, but I got it."

He nods and looks back into the gym. "Well, I'm staying for the dinner. You?"

"Nah. I fly out tomorrow. Gonna go back to the hotel and get some rest."

"So you ain't leaving here and going by my mama's house to see my sister?"

I can't stop the smile that spreads over my face. "I might make one stop before I turn in, yeah."

Chapter Twenty-Three

Takira

"Mama, I got this," I tell her, loading the dishwasher. "You can go on up."

"You sure?" she asks.

"Daddy went upstairs like an hour ago." I laugh. "Go be with your man."

"Your daddy hasn't washed a dish in forty years." Hands on hips, she rolls her eyes up to the ceiling. "You know that man leave the kitchen still chewing."

I nod, grinning and clearing the table of the dinner dishes.

"Ain't heard from Cliff," Mama says. "You suppose he all right?"

I freeze, my hand hovering over the stack of plates. I came this week because I love my brother, and if he needs me, I want to be here. That doesn't mean I'm not still pissed for how he handled our conversation last week.

"I'm sure he's fine." I give her a reassuring smile. "Myron would have called if something bad had gone down."

"Or Naz would have told you, I'm sure."

I can't fight off my smile. As much as I want to be here for Mama and for Cliff in case anything goes left, it was hard not driving over to Naz's hotel last night.

"He would have called, yeah," I agree. "Head on up, Mama."

She kisses my cheek and makes her way to the steps. I hear Daddy watching *Family Feud*. Surely my father is the only one recording episodes of that show.

I make quick work of the dishes and fend off restlessness. I don't want to bother Naz when he's at the dinner. He said he'd call when he left to let me know how it went. As much for distraction as anything else, I climb the steps up to the roof. It seemed so much bigger when I was eighteen. It was the best place to come dream and hope. Now it feels smaller and, with all us kids gone and never using it, neglected. Out of forgotten habit, I check the storage bench and grab an old blanket, then spread it on the cement floor. It's quiet up here, peaceful, and I wrap myself in memories—all the good times we had here as a family. Cliff was always on grill duty. I blink back tears as much for all that he lost as for how our conversation ended last week.

"Someone once told me the stars feel really close up here."

I sit up on the blanket, turning my head toward the stairs leading back into the house.

"Naz." I almost collapse with relief, glad to see him. Needing to hold him.

"Your mom let me up."

He crosses the roof and settles down beside me, stretching out on the blanket and pulling me onto his lap. I cuddle into him, disrupting his neatly tucked shirt by slipping my hand under it and dragging my palm over his warm skin. He kisses my hair and squeezes me tighter.

"Go ahead and ask," he says, his voice tinged with humor.

"How'd it go? With Cliff, I mean."

"He apologized to me."

I pull back, shock stretching my mouth open. "What? Cliff did?"

"Cliff did, and I'm sure you'll have one coming your way, too. Apparently he went to group and got some perspective."

The knot that's been in my stomach since I landed yesterday slowly loosens. "He's okay?"

"I think he's stronger than you give him credit for." Naz looks up at the stars, a small frown bending the thick line of his brows. "I think he's stronger than he gives himself credit for, but yeah. He seemed to be in a better place. I told him that was good since he and I will probably be related someday."

I go completely still in his arms, twisting to peer into his face with the light so dim.

"You said *what*?" I gasp, clutching a handful of his shirt reflexively.

"Oh, he was fine with it."

"What about if I'm fine with it? Maybe I'm not convinced you love me."

He lies back on the blanket, taking me with him and pulling me up until we're chest to chest and our faces are centimeters apart.

"I have ways of persuading you," he says, nibbling the line of my throat, his hand wandering up over the rise of my hip.

"Hmmm. I remember the last time we were up on this roof, all the persuading you did. Is that what I should expect?"

As he looks into my eyes, the laughter fades from his expression.

"You should expect that when the time is right," he says, his voice sure and fervent. "I'll ask you to marry me and refuse to settle for anything but yes."

The teasing smile dies on my lips as emotion warms my heart.

"You should expect that I'm going to spoil you and take care of you and remind you every day that I may not deserve you, but I'm never letting you go."

Tears gather at the corners of my eyes, and I let them fall.

"That night right here," he says, looking around the rooftop, "should have been our beginning, but instead everything went wrong. Everything in my life went right, except that. Except you."

And it changed everything, he's right. If Cliff had shown restraint, not punched that coach—if he hadn't let his resentment eat away at him, hadn't turned to drugs…his life could have been exactly as he'd envisioned. I could have avoided an army of frogs before I found my prince. But in the time apart from Naz, I grew into myself. Learned to accept my preferences, my desires. I learned to listen to my body and trust my instincts. I learned what a good friend is. I learned the difference between a good man and a bad one. What I was willing to accept and what I couldn't do without. Those years made me. They made Naz. Maybe the same forces that pushed us apart when we were so young, so untried, delivered me literally into Naz's arms when he was ready for me and I was ready for him.

"You know," I say, huddling deeper into him, "this was where I came to dream. It was the place where I felt closest to the stars. Where they felt brightest. It's where we first kissed." I pause to caress the strong planes of his face. "I used to think this rooftop held some kind of magic."

"And now?" he asks, his lips quirking with a smile.

"Now," I say, looking at the most beautiful boy who, despite all odds, became the love of my life and found his way back to me, "now I know it does."

Epilogue
Takira

One Year Later

Not again.

Thump thump whoosh

Thump thump whoosh

The sounds float up from Naz's basketball court outside of our bedroom window. He and Cliff have been at it for hours.

I'm seated on the edge of the bed—bathed, waxed, dolled up, and ready. I've been looking forward to this all day. All week, really, since I've been on set and have barely seen Naz. Little did I know that when he and Cliff made things right between them, it would be my own brother cock-blocking me. I love that he's staying with us here in LA for a few weeks while interviewing for a coaching job at a prestigious private high school, but enough is enough.

"Wanna go for another?" Cliff's shout climbs up through the open window.

I stomp over and lean out as far as I can go without falling or revealing how little I'm wearing.

"Hell no!" I yell, almost laughing when they both jump in surprise and glance up at me. "Game over. Find something to do for the rest of the night, Cliff. You had Naz long enough."

"Ewwww." Cliff slams the ball to the court and pretends to gag. "Don't tell me this is sex-related, 'cause I don't need to hear that shit about my little sister."

"Then I won't tell you." I laugh, shifting my gaze to Naz, who is grinning like a Cheshire cat with a bowl of cream. "But Naz has to come inside now. You two can play tomorrow."

Within minutes, Naz's footsteps are pounding up the stairs. Our bedroom door flings open, almost bouncing against the wall.

"You rang?" He kicks the door closed and prowls over to where I sit on the bed.

I roll my eyes and cross my arms under my breasts, pretending to be irritated but actually turned on by his bare chest, sinewy arms, massive shoulders, and the ridges of his eight-pack glistening with perspiration.

"It's a shame I had to." I mock-pout. "I thought you'd be here when I got home, ready to service me."

He leans in, hovers over me, forcing me to lay back on the bed. His eyes scour my pink bra, crotchless panties, garters, and kitten heels.

"I'm at your service now." He bends and leaves kisses along my throat.

I yelp, laughing when his sweat drips onto my chest. "You're nasty. Go take a shower."

"That's a great idea."

Before I have time to guess his intentions, he scoops me up and over his shoulder, walking toward the bathroom.

"No, you don't." I beat my fists against his broad back, laughing so hard I can hardly get the words out. "'Boy, if you—"

He slaps my ass, one arm behind my legs as I dangle over his shoulder. He uses his free hand to turn on the shower and walks us into the huge, tiled space under the spray. The shock of water makes me scream. When he sets me on my feet, I give up, letting the water soak my lingerie through.

"I bet you and Cliff would have been out there for another hour," I say, reaching for the body wash to soap up his chest, "if I hadn't called you in."

"I think you mean if you hadn't *booty-called* me in." He chuckles when I punch his chest with one soapy fist. "Cliff went out to grab some food. Your poor brother is probably scarred imagining all the things I'm doing to his baby sister tonight."

My hands slow in circles over his shoulder, wander down the corrugated muscles of his abdomen, and finally grip his dick with soap-slick palms. He bends until his lips rest right at my ear, whispering like it's a secret.

"I'm going to fuck you." He runs a finger between the cheeks of my ass, pressing one huge knuckle to the puckered entrance. "Here."

For a second, I don't respond, but shudder with the promise of something I enjoy so much with him. I slide my hand up and down his rigid length. "Your royal penis is clean, Your Highness."

"Not for long." He chuckles darkly, turning off the water. Standing in the shower, he unhooks the front closure of my fragile lace and silk bra, licking his lips when the straps slip down my arms and my breasts spill free. He tosses the bra to a corner of the shower.

"That's very expensive," I say, my voice hoarse, breathless. "Which you should know since you bought it. Don't be so careless."

"I won't be careless," he says, eyes riveted on my nipples hardening in the cool air after the water, "with you."

He unclips the garters from my panties and rolls down the sheer hose that cling to my legs. Removing the kitten heels, he tosses them and the hose and garters into a pile with my bra. The crotchless panties are next, and he goes down on his knees, lifting the front panel to suck my clit between his lips. I press one hand to the wall, nearly stumbling my knees go so weak. I sink my fingers into his head, pressing him deeper into the V of my thighs. My hips are rocking into the leisurely suction of his mouth when he pulls away and shucks off his basketball shorts.

"Naz, don't play with me," I growl as he stands to his full height, towering, naked and wet.

"We got time." Smiling, he takes my hand and leads me from the shower. He grabs a towel and dries me off, lingering on my breasts. Much more brusquely, he dries himself and walks back into the bedroom.

"Lie down," he orders, nodding toward our bed. I hesitate just to test him, giggling when his brows lift and he tilts his head toward the bed again. "I said lie down, Kira."

I settle onto the coolness of the sheets, my eyes fixed on the ceiling, and spread my legs. My heartbeat trips when cool air breezes across my heated flesh. He doesn't come to me right away, doesn't pounce on me with the urgency I'd half-expected since we haven't had much time together lately. He's taking his time—stretching out the anticipation. At the point when my nerves are drawn tight, he opens the drawer of the bedside table and pulls out a gold vibrator, one he bought for me a few weeks ago. I suck in a sharp breath and clench my hands at my sides.

"Okay, baby." His deep voice comes after several agonizing seconds. "Reach between your legs and hold yourself open for me."

I gulp, blinking furiously at the thought of what's about to happen. It's not the first time he's used a vibrator on me, and it's always intense in a way I never imagined it would be. I obey, raising my knees, spreading them, pulling myself open so cool air kisses the throbbing bud of nerves at the center of my body. Seconds tick by with nothing happening, and when I flick my glance to him, he's staring between my legs and biting his bottom lip.

He knows what it does to me when he looks at me like that. My bare toes curl into the bed.

"My pretty pussy," he rumbles. "Are you ready?"

I nod jerkily, beyond ready. Nerve-endings-stretched-thin ready.

The buzzing begins, and my inner muscles clench. My breath stutters as I wait for that first shock across my sensitive flesh. When it comes, when the mouth of the vibrator tugs on my clit, I jerk. My head snaps back, and one of my knees drops.

"No," he commands, pushing me knee back into place. "Up for me, baby. Should I go to the next setting?"

As much as I know it will torture me, I nod frantically, lost for words because it will also deliver unbearable pleasure. The buzzing gets louder as he adjusts the vibe, increasing the intensity. This time when it touches me, my knees spread wide open, yielding to the command of the instrument of torture. My hips buck. My neck arches, my mouth opens on a tearless sob. My fingers tremble around the lips I'm holding open, and I'm not sure how much longer I can do it when he adds a finger.

"Oh, god!" I scream. "Naz, no."

"Yes." His voice is hard. His breathing labored. I manage to open my eyes and find his—dark and filled with storm clouds. His mouth is slack with pleasure as he watches me. The vibrator on my clit. His finger, now another, now another filling me up and stroking in and out with increasing speed. I writhe on the bed, guttural sounds wrenched from my throat until it's raw. The tight knot building in my belly loosens, dispatching waves of pleasure to every inch of my body. My arms fall limply to my sides. Knees dropped open, my legs collapse as the orgasm possesses me. I gush, soaking my thighs and the sheet beneath me. I'm lost in a haze. The pleasure is a note sustained, drawn out as his fingers continue delving inside me, and even after the buzzing stops and he sets the vibrator aside, he rubs my clit with his thumb, spreading the wetness.

"You are so ready for me." His voice is gruff, his arms bracketing my head on the pillow. He notches his hips between my thighs.

"Yes." I rouse my limp arms and clutch his ass with both hands. "I need you inside."

"Oh, you're gonna get me inside. In that tight little ass."

A thrill, a shudder runs through me, and my asshole clenches in anticipation. Naz's dick is so big, anal was uncomfortable at first. I've done it before with relative ease.

But him?

It took a minute to adjust.

I don't have much time to process the promise of him taking me like that, *there* before his mouth is on my breasts.

"Naz, fuck me," I pant. "I'm ready."

"Obviously." He reaches between my legs, where the insides of my thighs and the duvet are soaked. "This is for me. I love your breasts."

His lips close around one nipple while he tugs at the other. My breath ratchets up, and my heartbeat, barely slowed, starts racing again.

"I'mma get to your ass." He pants, lifting me and plunging inside. "But just a little pussy first."

"Yes!" I slide my hands over his shoulders, around his neck, and pull him down to me. His mouth latches on to mine, our tongues sparring as the tempo of our bodies increases. I lock my ankles at the base of his spine, anchoring him to me. I'm on the verge of another orgasm when he pulls out.

"Dammit, Naz," I cry, my hips still moving in subtle, short jerks, seeking him.

He smiles above me, the masculine beauty of his face so arresting for a moment, I almost forget the way my inner muscles are clenching around air.

"I got you." He rains kisses over my cheeks and nose, soft feathering kisses punctuated by a bite at my throat. He loves to mark me, and I love carrying the little bruising reminders of our intimacy.

"Shit." He laughs. "I don't want Cliff seeing hickeys all over you. Don't want him to suspect I'm fucking his sister."

We both laugh at the preposterous joke. We've been living together for months and there's no missing how ravenous we are for each other.

No shame.

I don't deal in shame ever, and Naz never makes me feel it for anything I want. And I don't make him feel shame for what he wants. We just, as much as we can, give it to each other. There is a generosity to our lovemaking I've never experienced with anyone else. In one stroke, selfless. In the next, greedy. In every iteration, it's startlingly intimate and always powered by a love so deep and so real, it eclipses those old dreams, those first fantasies and ideals I held before. It is altogether new and more than my mind could have conceived.

"Naz, I need it." I reach between us to grab his dick.

"Don't I always take care of you?" His voice is shaded with confidence, love, desire.

"Yes."

And he does. I've never had to fake it with him because he ensures my pleasure. Always makes sure I've come at least once before he does. He promised he would spoil me, and I have a box full of jewelry, gifts from him. A closet full of clothes and shoes I try to convince him not to buy. There are fresh flowers delivered to the house every week. I chose a livelihood that often casts me in a supporting role, and I love it. Here, at home, though, with him, I'm the main character, and the way he spoils me most is with the extravagance of his love.

"On your knees." His command is a whisper underlined with steel. A shiver skitters over my spine.

I turn to face the headboard, pushing up onto all fours and spreading my legs so cool air breathes across the wet, hot flesh exposed by the position. My fists burrow into the mattress as he opens the drawer for the lube. The shock of coolness between my cheeks draws a gasp from me, and my thighs clench, anticipation crawling through my body. Not gonna lie, this shit hurts a little, but it's so worth it.

He covers me, his big body enfolding mine from behind, his broad, muscled torso at my back. His hands find me, first cupping my breast and tweaking the nipples, then wandering between my legs, tending to my clit. My breath hitches, and my body assumes the rhythm of his fingers. Leaving one hand on the bed for support, I knead my breast as his fingers stroke and push inside until another orgasm rocks me, so intense, I fall from my knees onto my belly and lie there, breaths choppy and heart sprinting in my chest.

"You're so good," he says at my ear. "Coming for me so much. It makes me hard when you come like that. Feel?"

He reaches under my stomach, pulls me back to my knees like I weigh nothing, and lets me feel the iron length of him at my ass. Involuntarily I arch my back, spread my legs, and offer myself to him.

"I'm gonna give it to you now," he says, caressing one cheek and then the other. "I love your ass, baby. I think about this pussy, my sweet girl all day. You are a constant distraction."

As he's talking, he rubs more lube across my asshole, and my breathing becomes erratic as he pulls my cheeks apart.

"I love you so much," he says, easing his dick into me slowly.

I clench around the tip, and he draws a sharp breath.

"Shit, baby. Let me in." He pushes on my shoulder so I fall forward, chest to the mattress. My ass is high in the air as he breaches me by thick inches, and I breathe through the initial discomfort, arching my back, opening as much as I can.

"Almost there," he grunts, his words choked as he pushes to the hilt.

A shout erupts from me, the shock of fullness I'm not sure I'll ever get used to. There's no room for anything but him. He presses one large hand to the small of my back, pinning me in place. With the other, he tugs my braids like a rein wrapped around his fist and starts riding.

Drawing back.

Ramming in.

Drawing back.

Ramming in.

Over and over, in and out, until the cadence of it becomes my heartbeat and a litany of encouragement, of thanks, of praise falls from my lips. Barely coherent, I fumble between my legs, clumsy but desperate to caress my swollen, soaked flesh.

"Kira!" he shouts, his thrusts frenzied and deep and hard in a way that shatters my control, splinters my composure. I scream into the mattress, my mouth full of sheets and bliss. My voice cracks, raw and hoarse as he breaks over me, loses himself inside me. So dominant and strong and hard, but with me, inside of me—vulnerable and undone when he comes.

"Baby," he chokes out, his hands tight at my hips. "I love you, Kira. I love you. God, I love you."

My body is wracked with sobs, not just of pleasure but of gratitude. How did this happen? How did we find this? Find each other for the first time and again? That person whose heart carries the key to yours—that soul that is a mirror reflecting yours. It's a connection not apparent to the naked eye, but unearthed, discovered in whispered conversations, in stolen kisses and urgent touches. Burrowing through layers of skin and bone and muscle until it strikes soul.

We hold each other in the wake of a violent storm, one that tossed us to and fro, broke us. He wraps himself around me from behind, and I'm limp and listless in his arms. Pushing the braids away from my neck, he leaves tender kisses there and over the curve of my shoulders.

"Did it hurt?" he rasps. "Are you okay?"

"It did hurt." I laugh, pressing my ass and back deeper into the granite line of his body. "A little at first, like it always does, but Jesus. It felt... I love it when you fuck me like that."

"I know." He reaches around and cups my breast, splays his hand possessively over my belly. I'm always amazed how hands so big can be so gentle.

"That vibrator." I turn my head to snare his eyes. "You doing that, controlling that is…" My breath stutters with the memory. "You always know."

"I'm always learning." He laughs. "Your responses tell me what to do, what feels good."

I clasp his arm curled around my waist, lifting his hand to kiss his palm. "I love you so much, Naz." A grin overtakes my face. "Even though you seem to prefer my brother's company to mine."

He flips me to my back and settles between my thighs, smiling down at me. "Your brother can still outshoot me, and you know how competitive I am. That shit is driving me crazy."

"So every night the two of you are down on that court playing for hours." I rub my foot along the hairs on his calf. "I'll be glad when he goes back to Texas."

He laughs, knowing I don't mean it. "He may be moving here. If he gets that job, your brother could be here in LA."

"Thank you for that." I reach up to trace his eyebrow, the fine rise of cheekbone. "For getting him that interview."

"I just cracked the door open." Naz shrugs powerful, naked shoulders. "His knowledge of the game and skill are what's pushing him through."

"You give me so much." I look up at him, pouring my adoration and respect and love into my eyes, praying he sees.

"You give me more just by breathing." He drops his head until our temples kiss. "By being with me. That's all I need."

I hold my hand up, studying the radiant cut pink diamond he placed there two months ago.

"You like it?" he asks unnecessarily because I just about fainted when he proposed. It's the most gorgeous ring I've ever seen.

"It could be made of coal and I'd love it because it means I get to spend the rest of my life with you."

"It could have been coal?" He reaches for my hand and slides the ring halfway up my finger. "Well, lemme get my money back."

I snatch my hand away and gently smack his shoulder, laughing.

"You ain't ever getting this ring off my finger. I'll wear it for the rest of my life. You spoil me, ya know?"

He looks at me, his smile dimming, his gaze brightening, intensifies like bright stars under the quarter moon.

"You deserve it," he says. "And I'm just getting started."

* * * *

Want more Takira & Naz?
Go to https://dl.bookfunnel.com/yh4poqt15u
to receive a bonus epilogue as soon as it's available!

* * * *

Also from 1001 Dark Nights and Kennedy Ryan, discover Queen Move.

Sign up for the 1001 Dark Nights Newsletter
and be entered to win a Tiffany Key necklace.

There's a contest every month!

Go to www.1001DarkNights.com to subscribe.

**As a bonus, all subscribers can download
FIVE FREE exclusive books!**

Discover 1001 Dark Nights Collection Nine

DRAGON UNBOUND by Donna Grant
A Dragon Kings Novella

NOTHING BUT INK by Carrie Ann Ryan
A Montgomery Ink: Fort Collins Novella

THE MASTERMIND by Dylan Allen
A Rivers Wilde Novella

JUST ONE WISH by Carly Phillips
A Kingston Family Novella

BEHIND CLOSED DOORS by Skye Warren
A Rochester Novella

GOSSAMER IN THE DARKNESS by Kristen Ashley
A Fantasyland Novella

THE CLOSE-UP by Kennedy Ryan
A Hollywood Renaissance Novella

DELIGHTED by Lexi Blake
A Masters and Mercenaries Novella

THE GRAVESIDE BAR AND GRILL by Darynda Jones
A Charley Davidson Novella

THE ANTI-FAN AND THE IDOL by Rachel Van Dyken
A My Summer In Seoul Novella

CHARMED BY YOU by J. Kenner
A Stark Security Novella

HIDE AND SEEK by Laura Kaye
A Blasphemy Novella

DESCEND TO DARKNESS by Heather Graham
A Krewe of Hunters Novella

BOND OF PASSION by Larissa Ione
A Demonica Novella

JUST WHAT I NEEDED by Kylie Scott
A Stage Dive Novella

Also from Blue Box Press

THE BAIT by C.W. Gortner and M.J. Rose

THE FASHION ORPHANS by Randy Susan Meyers and M.J. Rose

TAKING THE LEAP by Kristen Ashley
A River Rain Novel

SAPPHIRE SUNSET by Christopher Rice writing C. Travis Rice
A Sapphire Cove Novel

THE WAR OF TWO QUEENS by Jennifer L. Armentrout
A Blood and Ash Novel

THE MURDERS AT FLEAT HOUSE by Lucinda Riley

THE HEIST by C.W. Gortner and M.J. Rose

SAPPHIRE SPRING by Christopher Rice writing as C. Travis Rice
A Sapphire Cove Novel

MAKING THE MATCH by Kristen Ashley
A River Rain Novel

A LIGHT IN THE FLAME by Jennifer L. Armentrout
A Flesh and Fire Novel

Discover More Kennedy Ryan

Queen Move

From *Wall Street Journal*, *USA Today* Bestselling and RITA® Award winning Author, Kennedy Ryan, comes a captivating second chance romance like only she can deliver...

"The boy who always felt like mine is now the man I can't have."

Dig a little and you'll find photos of me in the bathtub with Ezra Stern. Get your mind out of the gutter. We were six months old.

Pry and one of us might confess we saved our first kiss for each other.

The most clumsy, wet, sloppy . . . spectacular thirty seconds of my adolescence.

Get into our business and you'll see two families, closer than blood, torn apart in an instant.

Twenty years later, my "awkward duckling" best friend from childhood, the boy no one noticed,

is a man no one can ignore.

Finer. Fiercer. Smarter.
Taken.

Tell me it's wrong.

Tell me the boy who always felt like mine is now the man I can't have.

When we find each other again, everything stands in our way--secrets, lies, promises.

But we didn't come this far to give up now.

And I know just the move to make if I want to make him mine.

Reel

Hollywood Renaissance
By Kennedy Ryan

Award-Winning Wall Street Journal bestselling author Kennedy Ryan launches a brand-new series with a Hollywood tale of wild ambition, artistic obsession, and unrelenting love.

One moment in the spotlight…

For months I stood by, an understudy waiting in the wings, preparing for my time to shine.

I never imagined *he* would watch in the audience that night.

Canon Holt.

Famous film director. Fascinating. Talented. *Fine.*

Before I could catch my breath, everything changed.

I went from backstage Broadway to center stage Hollywood.

From being unknown, to my name, Neevah Saint, on everyone's lips.

Canon casts me in a star-studded Harlem Renaissance biopic, catapulting me into another stratosphere.

But stars shine brightest in the dead of night.

Forbidden attraction, scandal and circumstances beyond my control jeopardize my dream.

Could this one shot—the role of a lifetime, the *love* of a lifetime—cost me everything?

* * * *

I rush from the wardrobe room, through the set, and out to the row of trailers. Olivia Ware, who plays Tilda, is only a few down from mine. I knock on the door and wait for her to invite me in.

"Sorry I'm late," I say, climbing the small set of steps. "I was in…"

The words dry up in my mouth when I see Canon sitting on the couch beside Livvie. They both look up from the script between them.

"I was in wardrobe," I finish. "Sorry to interrupt. I thought you wanted to run lines before—"

"I do," Livvie says. "I needed Canon to help ya girl get in touch with this next scene. It's tough, but I think I have it now."

"You got it. Don't worry." Canon stands, his head only a few inches shy of the ceiling in the compact trailer. "Let me know if you need anything else. I'm gonna go huddle with Jill before this next sequence."

He doesn't look at me, doesn't speak to me directly, but brushes past and walks out the door. I bite back a frustrated sigh. We have to wait. I get it, but does it have to be like this?

"Hey, Liv." I press my palms together in slightly pleading pose. "I want to ask Canon something about this next scene, too. You mind if I catch him?"

"Nah, ask while you can." She unties her robe to reveal one of Tilda's day dresses. "Everybody always wants a piece of him."

"Right," I say, smiling stiffly. "Be right back."

I open the door and hustle down the steps just in time to see Canon heading back toward set. Miraculously, there aren't a dozen people teeming around the trailers.

"Canon," I call, rushing to catch up.

He turns back to face me, looking damn good in his gray USC Film School sweatshirt and dark jeans. That beard is getting thicker. How would it feel if he kissed me now?

He tugs at the headphones that are always draped around his neck, his eyes cautious as I approach. "Neevah, hey. You need something?"

"Yeah, I do. I, um…" I toy with the belt of the terrycloth robe tied over my costume, fixing my eyes on the production team's fake sidewalk. "I just wondered if I imagined Thanksgiving."

I keep my voice low, but he still looks left and right, no doubt checking to see if anyone is around to hear. Grabbing my hand, he pulls me into one of the New York alleys they fabricated for the set, a tight channel between the sides of two fake buildings. He leans against one wall and I face him, leaning against the other.

"No, you didn't imagine it," he finally says, his hands shoved into his pockets. "We just can't repeat it."

"Ever?" I squeak.

"What'd I tell you?" His smile is a slow-burning secret. "Not yet."

"You think you're being discreet by avoiding me, but I think it draws attention that you give everyone else their notes directly except me. All my notes come through Kenneth."

"I don't care if people speculate about that. That's not the only reason I don't want a lot of contact with you."

It stings, those words. Even knowing what's behind them, hearing him actually voice what I've suspected doesn't feel great.

"Then why?" I ask, keeping my chin and eyes level. I'm determined not to get emotional because that's the last thing he wants and that's not who I am. I never let personal stuff get in the way of a performance, of the work, but I've also never felt like this about someone I worked with.

"It's for me," he says, not looking away. "It's so I can focus. You distract me."

A huge grin spreads across my face.

"Don't." He chuckles and narrows his eyes. "Do not."

"I'm a distraction, huh?" I take the few steps separating us until only a heartbeat fits between our chests. The alley walls close in on us and I'm surrounded by the clean, masculine scent of him.

The humor fades from his expression, and he links our fingers at our sides. "We need to wait."

Disappointment pierces the lust and longing suffusing my senses. "Until we wrap?"

He bends to drop a kiss on my forehead, slides his lips down to briefly take mine, the beard a soft scrape against my cheek. I grip his elbows, not wanting him to pull away, to go back to ignoring me. Just beyond this fake alley and deep shadows is the set and the cast and the crew and the real world. And this…we…are not happening there yet. And I just want a few more seconds in *this* world where we are, even if the only real thing here is us.

"Did you really need help for this next scene?" he whispers in my ear, his wide palm running down my back and resting just above the curve of my ass.

"Yes. In this next scene, can you tell me…" I glance up mock-seriously through my lashes. "What's my motivation?"

He flashes that too-rare grin, white and wolfish, confident, bordering on cocky.

"You'll be fine." He squeezes my hip. "That's my girl."

And while I'm still relishing that, he turns and walks away.

About Kennedy Ryan

A RITA® and Audie® Award winner, *USA Today* bestselling author Kennedy Ryan writes for women from all walks of life, empowering them and placing them firmly at the center of each story and in charge of their own destinies. Her heroes respect, cherish, and lose their minds for the women who capture their hearts. To date, six of her novels have been optioned for television/film and her writings have been featured in *Chicken Soup for the Soul, USA Today, Entertainment Weekly, Glamour, Cosmopolitan, TIME,* Om agazine, and many others. The co-founder of LIFT 4 Autism, an annual charitable book auction, she is a wife to her lifetime lover and mother to an extraordinary son.

Find out more about Kennedy at https://kennedyryanwrites.com.

Discover 1001 Dark Nights

COLLECTION ONE
FOREVER WICKED by Shayla Black ~ CRIMSON TWILIGHT by
Heather Graham ~ CAPTURED IN SURRENDER by Liliana Hart ~
SILENT BITE: A SCANGUARDS WEDDING by Tina Folsom ~
DUNGEON GAMES by Lexi Blake ~ AZAGOTH by Larissa Ione ~
NEED YOU NOW by Lisa Renee Jones ~ SHOW ME, BABY by Cherise
Sinclair~ ROPED IN by Lorelei James ~ TEMPTED BY MIDNIGHT by
Lara Adrian ~ THE FLAME by Christopher Rice ~ CARESS OF
DARKNESS by Julie Kenner

COLLECTION TWO
WICKED WOLF by Carrie Ann Ryan ~ WHEN IRISH EYES ARE
HAUNTING by Heather Graham ~ EASY WITH YOU by Kristen Proby
~ MASTER OF FREEDOM by Cherise Sinclair ~ CARESS OF
PLEASURE by Julie Kenner ~ ADORED by Lexi Blake ~ HADES by
Larissa Ione ~ RAVAGED by Elisabeth Naughton ~ DREAM OF YOU
by Jennifer L. Armentrout ~ STRIPPED DOWN by Lorelei James ~
RAGE/KILLIAN by Alexandra Ivy/Laura Wright ~ DRAGON KING
by Donna Grant ~ PURE WICKED by Shayla Black ~ HARD AS STEEL
by Laura Kaye ~ STROKE OF MIDNIGHT by Lara Adrian ~ ALL
HALLOWS EVE by Heather Graham ~ KISS THE FLAME by
Christopher Rice~ DARING HER LOVE by Melissa Foster ~ TEASED
by Rebecca Zanetti ~ THE PROMISE OF SURRENDER by Liliana Hart

COLLECTION THREE
HIDDEN INK by Carrie Ann Ryan ~ BLOOD ON THE BAYOU by
Heather Graham ~ SEARCHING FOR MINE by Jennifer Probst ~
DANCE OF DESIRE by Christopher Rice ~ ROUGH RHYTHM by
Tessa Bailey ~ DEVOTED by Lexi Blake ~ Z by Larissa Ione ~
FALLING UNDER YOU by Laurelin Paige ~ EASY FOR KEEPS by
Kristen Proby ~ UNCHAINED by Elisabeth Naughton ~ HARD TO
SERVE by Laura Kaye ~ DRAGON FEVER by Donna Grant ~
KAYDEN/SIMON by Alexandra Ivy/Laura Wright ~ STRUNG UP by
Lorelei James ~ MIDNIGHT UNTAMED by Lara Adrian ~ TRICKED
by Rebecca Zanetti ~ DIRTY WICKED by Shayla Black ~ THE ONLY
ONE by Lauren Blakely ~ SWEET SURRENDER by Liliana Hart

COLLECTION FOUR

ROCK CHICK REAWAKENING by Kristen Ashley ~ ADORING INK by Carrie Ann Ryan ~ SWEET RIVALRY by K. Bromberg ~ SHADE'S LADY by Joanna Wylde ~ RAZR by Larissa Ione ~ ARRANGED by Lexi Blake ~ TANGLED by Rebecca Zanetti ~ HOLD ME by J. Kenner ~ SOMEHOW, SOME WAY by Jennifer Probst ~ TOO CLOSE TO CALL by Tessa Bailey ~ HUNTED by Elisabeth Naughton ~ EYES ON YOU by Laura Kaye ~ BLADE by Alexandra Ivy/Laura Wright ~ DRAGON BURN by Donna Grant ~ TRIPPED OUT by Lorelei James ~ STUD FINDER by Lauren Blakely ~ MIDNIGHT UNLEASHED by Lara Adrian ~ HALLOW BE THE HAUNT by Heather Graham ~ DIRTY FILTHY FIX by Laurelin Paige ~ THE BED MATE by Kendall Ryan ~ NIGHT GAMES by CD Reiss ~ NO RESERVATIONS by Kristen Proby ~ DAWN OF SURRENDER by Liliana Hart

COLLECTION FIVE

BLAZE ERUPTING by Rebecca Zanetti ~ ROUGH RIDE by Kristen Ashley ~ HAWKYN by Larissa Ione ~ RIDE DIRTY by Laura Kaye ~ ROME'S CHANCE by Joanna Wylde ~ THE MARRIAGE ARRANGEMENT by Jennifer Probst ~ SURRENDER by Elisabeth Naughton ~ INKED NIGHTS by Carrie Ann Ryan ~ ENVY by Rachel Van Dyken ~ PROTECTED by Lexi Blake ~ THE PRINCE by Jennifer L. Armentrout ~ PLEASE ME by J. Kenner ~ WOUND TIGHT by Lorelei James ~ STRONG by Kylie Scott ~ DRAGON NIGHT by Donna Grant ~ TEMPTING BROOKE by Kristen Proby ~ HAUNTED BE THE HOLIDAYS by Heather Graham ~ CONTROL by K. Bromberg ~ HUNKY HEARTBREAKER by Kendall Ryan ~ THE DARKEST CAPTIVE by Gena Showalter

COLLECTION SIX

DRAGON CLAIMED by Donna Grant ~ ASHES TO INK by Carrie Ann Ryan ~ ENSNARED by Elisabeth Naughton ~ EVERMORE by Corinne Michaels ~ VENGEANCE by Rebecca Zanetti ~ ELI'S TRIUMPH by Joanna Wylde ~ CIPHER by Larissa Ione ~ RESCUING MACIE by Susan Stoker ~ ENCHANTED by Lexi Blake ~ TAKE THE BRIDE by Carly Phillips ~ INDULGE ME by J. Kenner ~ THE KING by Jennifer L. Armentrout ~ QUIET MAN by Kristen Ashley ~ ABANDON by Rachel Van Dyken ~ THE OPEN DOOR by Laurelin Paige~ CLOSER by Kylie Scott ~ SOMETHING JUST LIKE THIS by Jennifer Probst ~ BLOOD NIGHT by Heather Graham ~ TWIST OF

FATE by Jill Shalvis ~ MORE THAN PLEASURE YOU by Shayla Black ~ WONDER WITH ME by Kristen Proby ~ THE DARKEST ASSASSIN by Gena Showalter

COLLECTION SEVEN
THE BISHOP by Skye Warren ~ TAKEN WITH YOU by Carrie Ann Ryan ~ DRAGON LOST by Donna Grant ~ SEXY LOVE by Carly Phillips ~ PROVOKE by Rachel Van Dyken ~ RAFE by Sawyer Bennett ~ THE NAUGHTY PRINCESS by Claire Contreras ~ THE GRAVEYARD SHIFT by Darynda Jones ~ CHARMED by Lexi Blake ~ SACRIFICE OF DARKNESS by Alexandra Ivy ~ THE QUEEN by Jen Armentrout ~ BEGIN AGAIN by Jennifer Probst ~ VIXEN by Rebecca Zanetti ~ SLASH by Laurelin Paige ~ THE DEAD HEAT OF SUMMER by Heather Graham ~ WILD FIRE by Kristen Ashley ~ MORE THAN PROTECT YOU by Shayla Black ~ LOVE SONG by Kylie Scott ~ CHERISH ME by J. Kenner ~ SHINE WITH ME by Kristen Proby

COLLECTION EIGHT
DRAGON REVEALED by Donna Grant ~ CAPTURED IN INK by Carrie Ann Ryan ~ SECURING JANE by Susan Stoker ~ WILD WIND by Kristen Ashley ~ DARE TO TEASE by Carly Phillips ~ VAMPIRE by Rebecca Zanetti ~ MAFIA KING by Rachel Van Dyken ~ THE GRAVEDIGGER'S SON by Darynda Jones ~ FINALE by Skye Warren ~ MEMORIES OF YOU by J. Kenner ~ SLAYED BY DARKNESS by Alexandra Ivy ~ TREASURED by Lexi Blake ~ THE DAREDEVIL by Dylan Allen ~ BOND OF DESTINY by Larissa Ione ~ MORE THAN POSSESS YOU by Shayla Black ~ HAUNTED HOUSE by Heather Graham ~ MAN FOR ME by Laurelin Paige ~ THE RHYTHM METHOD by Kylie Scott ~ JONAH BENNETT by Tijan ~ CHANGE WITH ME by Kristen Proby ~ THE DARKEST DESTINY by Gena Showalter

Discover Blue Box Press
TAME ME by J. Kenner ~ TEMPT ME by J. Kenner ~ DAMIEN by J. Kenner ~ TEASE ME by J. Kenner ~ REAPER by Larissa Ione ~ THE SURRENDER GATE by Christopher Rice ~ SERVICING THE TARGET by Cherise Sinclair ~ THE LAKE OF LEARNING by Steve Berry and M.J. Rose ~ THE MUSEUM OF MYSTERIES by Steve Berry and M.J. Rose ~ TEASE ME by J. Kenner ~ FROM BLOOD AND ASH by Jennifer L. Armentrout ~ QUEEN MOVE by Kennedy Ryan ~ THE

HOUSE OF LONG AGO by Steve Berry and M.J. Rose ~ THE BUTTERFLY ROOM by Lucinda Riley ~ A KINGDOM OF FLESH AND FIRE by Jennifer L. Armentrout ~ THE LAST TIARA by M.J. Rose ~ THE CROWN OF GILDED BONES by Jennifer L. Armentrout ~ THE MISSING SISTER by Lucinda Riley ~ THE END OF FOREVER by Steve Berry and M.J. Rose ~ THE STEAL by C. W. Gortner and M.J. Rose ~ CHASING SERENITY by Kristen Ashley ~ A SHADOW IN THE EMBER by Jennifer L. Armentrout

On Behalf of 1001 Dark Nights,

Liz Berry, M.J. Rose, and Jillian Stein would like to thank ~

Steve Berry
Doug Scofield
Benjamin Stein
Kim Guidroz
Social Butterfly PR
Asha Hossain
Chris Graham
Chelle Olson
Kasi Alexander
Jessica Saunders
Dylan Stockton
Kate Boggs
Richard Blake
and Simon Lipskar

Made in United States
North Haven, CT
08 August 2022

22425960R00095